I0598294

# Governess for a Week

## by

## Barbara Jean Miller

This is a work of fiction. Names, characters, places, and incidents are either the product of the author's imagination or are used fictitiously, and any resemblance to actual persons living or dead, business establishments, events, or locales, is entirely coincidental.

**Governess for a Week**

Cover Art by *Jennifer Greeff*

The Wild Rose Press, Inc.
PO Box 708
Adams Basin, NY 14410-0708
Visit us at www.thewildrosepress.com

Publishing History
First Edition, 2023
Trade Paperback ISBN 978-1-5092-5132-2
Digital ISBN 978-1-5092-5133-9


Published in the United States of America

"And you don't see the injustice of paying an actress as much for an evening of entertainment as you would pay a poor governess for a year's labor?"

"It's not the money."

"Easy for you to say since you have it to throw away. I have a mother to support."

"But people know you now as my fiancée. How can I present you to them as a governess? They would recognize you."

"You did not, until I spoke. Frobisher still does not realize it."

"It was your voice." He ducked his head again, unable to look at her, she surmised, when he knew her cause was just.

"They will never see me. *You* need never see me." She gestured with her hands. "Besides, I have two faces, one for the children and one I used to wear when I was in society, the one you saw last night. No one need ever see that face again." If only she could convince him of her ability to disappear, he might let her stay.

Wyle looked at her earnest sweet face and knew a wave of regret. How could such a beauty condemn herself to obscurity? Major Greenway had been announced missing after the battle of San Sebastian, the same one in which Wyle had been wounded. Greenway was thought dead until his body was not found. Then there were rumors of desertion or treason. "Just leave me."

"But what about Charlotte and Henry? They asked me if I would stay forever."

"And I suppose you said you would."

"That would be stupid. I said it was up to them."

**Praise for Barbara Jean Miller**

"The secondary characters were phenomenal and well developed. They played a big part in the storyline. There are many twists and turns before the reader has any idea how the book will end. The happily-ever-after still held surprises for me and it did not turn out as I expected. I loved this book and highly recommend it to everyone."

~*The Romance Studio*

# Dedication

For my devoted writing friends,
Linda Ciletti and Judith Gallagher

Chapter One

*London, March 1814*

Marian Greenway pulled her old gray cloak tighter and gazed out the window of the hired carriage as it wove its way down a crowded Oxford Street that Saturday evening. It was still light enough for her to recognize familiar houses where she had once been a guest. She turned her face away when they drew near the house her parents used to lease. That was in the past and she had best forget it. She had not wanted to take a position in London because she had known so many people here, but she was not likely to encounter them while walking her charges in the square, wearing her gown of somber gray. Even if she did, they would never recognize her. Governesses were as good as invisible. It was as though the pretty young heiress had died four years ago, and the real Marian was a different person altogether.

There was one problem. Even though she was twenty-two, old for the marriage mart, she still looked far too young to be a governess. She dashed away the stray tear that threatened to bring a deluge. She could not appear to her new employer with red eyes. She had to think about the children to be cared for. She felt the letter in her reticule. Too dark now to read it again, but she did not need to. After reciting back to her all her accomplishments which he wanted her to pass on to her charges, her new employer's secretary had said she would do, much in the manner of her father speaking about a new hunter.

She wondered how it would be, working for a man with no wife in residence, a widower. She had heard his French-bred wife had died in Italy, there for a cure without him. Marian had also heard about Captain David Armstead, Earl of Wyle, during her come-out year. A soldier, an artillery officer. Her father had taught her how to deal with that type up to a point. She had even met Wyle in Spain, but he would never remember her. She thought the moment remote enough to slip from a man's memory.

By the time the carriage turned into Grosvenor Square she felt composed again and had a coin ready for the coachman. The house looked three times the width of most of the town residences, with a floor below street level for the kitchens and four floors towering above. Years before, Marian had been a guest here when she and her mother had attended a musical given by one of the aunts. The earl had been at war so would not remember her from that event.

To her surprise, no less than two footmen dashed out of the house to let down the steps and help her descend. Her trunks were in the antechamber almost before she knew what was happening, and she confronted the freezing disapproval of the portly butler.

"Lord Wyle is expecting me," she said, trying to banish the mist of tears with precise enunciation but still hearing the milky evidence of their threat in her voice.

The butler turned ponderously and led her to a door down the main hall on the left, but just then it sprang open and a tall man in evening dress stepped out. "Where the devil have you been?" He limped over to stare intently into her face, his blue gaze slicing through her like a knife. Wyle had dressed for a formal evening and she supposed her arrival would now permit him to go out on the town.

Their faces were only inches apart, and she had the oddest notion he meant to kiss her. She resisted the impulse to back away. It wasn't that he appeared repulsive even with the scar near his hairline. Far from it. That gun-metal black hair and those compelling blue eyes made him all too appealing. And also those dents at the corners of his firm mouth hinted his smile would be heart-wrenching if he ever gave it. Was he short-sighted or merely rude?

"I said I would arrive at—"

"Very well, never mind," he said as he grabbed her hand. "You will do, but there isn't a moment to lose." He then dragged her back toward the front of the house, up the grand stairs, and into a room on the second floor that looked far too elaborate to belong to a governess. She felt amazed at the alacrity of their ascent since he seemed to suffer from a stiff knee.

"Here is the dress you are to wear tonight." He gestured toward a sleek gray satin gown on the bed. "I see you've brought your trunks, but I want you to wear what I chose."

"Tonight? But what—"

"There is no time to rehearse anything. Just act naturally. The first guests will be arriving in a moment. Ah, here is your maid, Susan, to help you. Change now or I will help you as well."

Wyle exited then, leaving her to stare open-mouthed at the girl still bent in a deep curtsy. The slight maid stood

3

up, her brown eyes concerned.

"What is going on?" Marian asked.

"A dinner party, miss, with just a few of his lordship's particular friends and his relatives." The maid smiled, then came to help Marian off with her cloak.

"But, I mean, a woman in my position is not expected to attend a dinner party."

The girl now shook out the shimmer of gray silk that passed for a dress as though to tempt her. "Please, miss, if you are not ready in time he will blame me, and I can't stand it when he is in a rage with me."

"Oh, very well, but Lord Wyle has made a grave error." She unbuttoned her cuffs and let the maid undo the back of her black wool dress.

"I know, miss. Mr. Trumby, the butler, tried to tell him so, but he never listens, not even to his secretary, Mr. Hill."

"But it is Mr. Hill who hired me."

"Indeed, miss? That is a shocker. But Lord Wyle does take these starts into his head, and there is no dissuading him."

So she regarded Wyle as delusional. Perhaps the head wound. Glad to have her assessment of the situation confirmed, Marian quickly discarded her shift and washed up. Mr. Hill's letter had been so stuffy about her requirements, she had assumed him to be a serious man, but it now came home to her that she didn't know if she could trust Hill either. Clearly Wyle expected to turn her into some sort of hostess, and she doubted the propriety of the whole situation. Still he had other women servants in the house. But she felt too tired to fight with him tonight. That could wait until morning. She would make him sorry for trampling over her with such an assumption.

The maid dumped a gauze shift and then the shimmer of silk over her head, and Marian gasped when she looked at herself in the mirror.

"You are that lovely, miss."

"Is there a fichu with this dress?"

"No, miss, only what his lordship laid out."

"I cannot wear this," Marian said. She caught a panicky look on the maid's face and felt sorry for the girl who would be blamed if Marian backed out. Then she thought back to her come out, when she had worn a dress cut almost as low. She'd been such a young fool in those days.

"Perhaps a shawl?" she asked, mesmerized by the sheen of the fabric as it revealed a figure perhaps too thin.

Marian grabbed the jacquard silk shawl Susan unearthed from the wardrobe. It wasn't much help, but it would have to do. She must be insane to accede to Lord Wyle's wishes. She should simply leave. But night had fallen, she had no money to hire a room nor means to get to an inn, and she felt tired. Then her stomach growled. Hungry too. She might get nothing more from the man than a decent dinner and a night's rest, but she would have that, by God.

The maid seemed to have some talent with a brush and comb and helped her arrange her hair into a simple fall that would curl around her neck and make the lack of her pearls not so noticeable. A single white rosebud plucked from a vase would serve as ornament for her hair. But the girl then produced a necklace that she could swear contained real diamonds. What did this mean? She felt like someone in a poorly written fairy tale.

When she swept down the stairs, she could feel the heightened color in her cheeks. A footman with a stony face conducted her to the room from which Wyle had come to greet her, at the back of the first floor. As she recalled, the drawing room and music room. She entered and all eyes turned toward her. Just such an entrance as she had always wanted to make. She had not garnered this much attention since her presentation. Wondering if she still had her old poise, she tilted her head up and smiled. The curious looks softened, and then Wyle strode across the floor to take her arm. She could almost imagine him as her escort, and he seemed delighted to see her. Wyle did look pleased—no—relieved. But why?

"Are you cold?" he whispered, which seemed an intimate question.

"No, in fact it seems excessively warm in here."

"Then you won't be needing this," he said, slipping the wrap off her shoulders and tossing it behind a chair. She felt as though he had exposed her and barely managed not to flinch.

"Come and meet my family. By the way, what is your name again?"

"Marian Greenway."

"Aunt Flora, Aunt Alva, everyone, this is Mary Green, my fiancée."

For a moment she thought she had not heard Wyle correctly. He had surely not heard her. An artillery officer might be hard of hearing from the constant shelling. But there could be no excuse for the second half of his statement other than insanity.

As the congratulations poured over her from his aunts and cousins, she must have looked confused. She wondered what game he played, introducing her to his family in this absurd manner. They were tall, all of them, the women robust and the men jovial. Most were dark-haired and blue-eyed like Wyle.

Even though part of her wanted to slap him and demand an explanation, she simply could not be rude to them. Perhaps he was insane and they were all there to humor him. Yet their well wishes seemed genuine, except for the glare of Cousin Isabelle, a slight blonde, who hung back and scrutinized her with cold green eyes.

"Now, let us go in to dinner." He snatched her arm back from his cousin Edward, Alva's son, and conducted her into the large dining room across the hall.

Marian found herself seated on Wyle's left. "What the devil is this about?" she whispered.

"Had you arrived on time I might have been able to fill you in."

"So this is my fault?" She draped her napkin over her lap but had difficulty keeping it there on the silk.

"No, it is mine for letting Frobisher arrange anything for me. I should have made a way to meet you ahead of time."

"Who is Frobisher?"

"The man who hired you."

She now felt as though his insanity was infectious. "But Mr. Hill did."

He gave her an impatient look and she thought he had not heard her again.

"Can this wait? We have an engagement dinner to get through."

"But—"

"Then we will discuss your fee later, if you give satisfaction."

"Satisfaction?" Anger now added to the flush in her

7

cheeks. How dare he say such a thing to her?

"Come now, it's only for an evening. I mean to pay you well."

"You are mad, absolutely mad."

"So my men always told me. Then humor me."

By then, the aunts and cousins had resolved the seating and Marian's attention was claimed by Wyle's cousin Morris, Isabelle's son, who seemed such a polite young man he sapped the ire she had in the making for her employer. And why bother to learn their names if this was only for a night? More to the point, what did Wyle mean by calling her his fiancée and then saying it was only for an evening? Morris asked her where she was from, and Wyle grimaced at her as though trying to silence her.

"From Northampton. My father's estate is near Sudbury."

Now Wyle positively glared at her, but she shrugged as though it did not matter. He had discomposed her and she meant to have her revenge. Flora nodded with approval, and Marian recalled she had met both Flora and Alva at the musicale. The earl's wife had still been alive and had played the harp.

The dinner proved excellent and she let no dish get past her, not from the salmon in wine sauce to the buttered new peas. She would have wished to linger over the fruit and nut dishes as she studied the still-lifes that decorated the mint green walls. She could see that once the ladies moved into the drawing room she would have to run a gantlet of female relatives while the men chased dinner with a glass of port. And they were not all smiling. Cousin Isabelle was assessing the cost of her gown and comparing it unfavorably to the one her own daughter

Sophie wore.

After they paraded across the hall again and found seats in the wood-paneled drawing room, Marian studied the gilt-framed portraits on the walls as she reflected on how much less convenient the house appeared for family gatherings than for crowds. Except for the dining room, the entire first floor was intended for large entertainments. Presumably the drawing room opened onto a ballroom or other large salon on the same side of the house, but for a family party there was too much traveling to suit her. But what did it matter?

Wyle's Aunt Flora sailed toward her like a frigate about to do battle and took the seat next to her. "How wonderful to see you again. Is your acquaintance with my nephew of long standing?"

Marian took a moment to compose herself and determined to stick as close to the thin fabric of truth as she could. "You remember me after all these years? Wyle and I met in Spain."

"So, love at first sight!" Flora seemed genuinely entranced.

Marian smiled sadly at her own plight but said, "More a matter of him needing a keeper."

"That is so true. Just how did you meet?"

"We were introduced by a mutual acquaintance. Let me think who." She tapped her finger against her chin.

"Lieutenant Frobisher, no doubt." Flora shook her head.

"Yes, Frobisher. Do you know him?"

"Unfortunately, yes. No matter. I knew your mother and your father. Major Greenway, is he not?"

Marian jumped. "You know them well?"

"Yes, there are those who said your mother could

have done better, but she loved your father, quite a handsome man in his day. David got your name wrong. Did you know he is slightly deaf in one ear from the war?"

"That explains so much. Was he badly wounded?"

"Yes, in the head, also his leg and hand. No more than usual for an artillery officer."

Aunt Flora saw someone at the pianoforte and got up to see who, leaving Marian feeling instant sympathy for Wyle. She must stop this. She always felt sorry for people and it got her in trouble all the time.

Sophie prepared to give an impromptu recital at her mother's urging. How odd that Isabelle should be the one to inadvertently rescue her from further questions. The girl played quite well and Marian applauded each piece along with the other ladies. She attended so closely she must not have noticed the entrance of the men, for she jumped when Wyle said, "How goes it?" over her shoulder.

To her credit she did not turn at the question whispered in her ear.

"Do you realize your Aunt Flora knows my parents?"

"How is that possible?" he whispered fiercely.

"We were in society."

"Well, no mending that now. Who is your family?"

"Major John Greenway and Lady Elizabeth Parkening."

Wyle's face clouded. "Greenway from the Peninsula?"

"Yes, but he is reported missing now. I presume he's been captured by the French."

"How could his daughter have come to this?"

She pulled back and looked sideways at him. "That is a very impertinent question."

"But I want to know."

"And I want to know why it is so important for you to be engaged just for one evening."

"Simple. I must convince my relatives I am getting on with my life or they—especially Aunt Alva—will spend all their time matching me with eligible women."

"That scarcely seems reason enough for such a charade," she whispered. "What will they think when you announce the end of the engagement?"

"Well, I won't. At least not for a good long time. I suppose you will expect some consideration for that."

"I am in the habit of earning my keep."

"Oh, really?" He arched his right eyebrow.

"I mean it is absurd that you would pay for… This whole situation is absurd."

"But you agreed to it."

"Never," she said as Sophie finished with a flourish and Marian applauded.

He held a finger to his lips even though he had been the one talking over Sophie's playing and attracting Isabelle's glare. The girl's gown was a bronze silk too old for her tender years, but she had her mother's flaxen hair and beautiful green eyes, so much could be forgiven the dress. Now Marian had to bear the scrutiny of all the people she had just met. To do them credit, they sent her mostly good-natured glances, especially the men. Aunt Flora seemed content, but Aunt Alva looked puzzled. Cousin Isabelle picked Marian apart with needle-sharp looks.

When Sophie returned to her seat, Aunt Flora vowed she would like more music and asked Marian if she would oblige them. When she stood, Wyle gave a start as though to protect her, or perhaps hold her back. Didn't he realize anything would be easier for her than conversing with relatives about him when she didn't know the slightest thing? Or did he expect her not to know proper music? It had been in her credentials. Had he not even read them?

She found some suitable pieces in the music portfolio and Cousin Bertram volunteered to come and turn pages for her. She knew him for Flora's son by his smiling good looks. Even though Wyle seemed insane, most of his family were nice, especially to an interloper they did not even know. If she really were engaged to Wyle she might be cutting a distant relative out of a position as his wife. Ah, so that was Isabelle's problem. She wanted Wyle for Sophie, who must be through several generations a second cousin. As Marian played she constructed the family tree in her mind. It was not unlike the military rosters her father used to have her copy out.

Finally the tea tray arrived and Marian brought a foreshortened end to her current piece with a sigh of relief. She thought she had accredited herself well, but Wyle had a definite dent between his eyebrows. Some men were never happy. Of course if he had trouble hearing, he would have no way of knowing how well or badly she played. It might have sounded like a great cacophony to him.

She looked up and smiled at Wyle, who gave her a relieved nod. As the matriarch of the family, Aunt Flora poured tea for everyone. She knew how everyone took their tea. When Marian went for a cup, Flora squinted her eyes as though she consulted some supernatural medium.

"Milk. No sugar."

"How did you know?"

"That is how your father drank his tea. So just a guess." Her fading blue eyes shone.

Marian found herself smiling. "But how did you remember that?"

"I am too old to have much skill at anything but remembering now. I find I have a facility for it."

Marian took a gulp as she studied the comment— idle chatter or a warning? So hard to tell. Isabelle came to sit beside her, looking ready for a confrontation. Since her last name was Armstead like Wyle, and so were her children's, Morris and Sophie, Marian thought Isabelle an in-law with the name having come down some paternal branch of the family. Morris Armstead must be in line for the title if anything happened to Wyle or his son.

"This engagement seems very sudden."

"In wartime everything seems to happen so fast," Marian replied. "Wyle may be called back to service at any moment."

"Possibly leaving you with child."

Since they were not yet wed, her implication cut, and Alva's head came up as though she had heard it. Marian faced Isabelle and said, "Two children, actually, Henry and Charlotte. Someone must take responsibility for them while he is gone."

"I would think his family would be able to provide a place for them if he is so concerned."

She could see Alva whispering to Morris. Goodness, did they mean to rescue her?

Cousin Morris came to loom over them with the same dent between his brows as Wyle. Tall but still a student, if she guessed his age right.

"Mother, if I recall, you said raising Sophie and me had almost been the death of you. You are in no frame to care for children. My aunts are too busy. I'm sure Wyle has made the right decision."

"You know nothing about it, Morris," Isabelle snapped. "If anything happens to young Henry, you would be the earl, so it's time you thought of family and responsibility also."

"You mean if anything happens to both Henry and Wyle," Marian corrected.

"Yes, of course. But if Wyle insists on throwing his life away in the army, what are we to do about it?"

Morris shook his head and sent Marian a speaking glance. "Now that Miss Greenway will be marrying Wyle, nothing will happen to Henry or Charlotte."

"Still, I think—"

Alva Ridgeway loomed over them. "That young scamp Henry should be sent to school. We shipped Edward off when he was no more than seven. He turned out fine."

Morris laughed and turned to his cousin. "Did you turn out fine, Edward?"

Alva's son left off talking to Sophie. "I survived school, and that is all that one can hope. As for learning anything, I was too busy watching my back."

"Henry will not be going to school for some time, and that is final." They had not seen Wyle come up behind the crowd around Marian.

"But to leave them with a stranger…" Isabelle said.

"Is quite my affair." He planted his right hand firmly on the arm of Marian's chair, and she noticed a scar between his thumb and index finger.

"I'm sure you will do just as you please. We must be off. We have another engagement tonight."

The exodus of these three guests seemed to give the others the idea they should depart. Ten minutes later, Wyle saw the last of his relatives out and came back into the drawing room to find his hired fiancée sipping a final cup of tea.

"That must be cold by now."

"Still, it is very refreshing after the dinner wine and the champagne. Besides I need my wits about me."

"Why? Afraid I may cheat you?"

She put the cup and saucer down with finality. "No, I am afraid I may forget some of the things I have been storing up to say to you."

He smiled as he limped toward her, hands behind his back. "Such as?"

"How dare you presume to treat me like some sort of ornament? I felt almost as though…as though…"

"Go on." He smiled wickedly.

"Never mind. I came here to do an honest job. I did not expect to be thrown into a lunatic asylum."

"Well, I know my relatives are odd, but it wasn't as bad as all that."

"I meant *you*."

"I thought my request reasonable enough, and here is your payment, three hundred guineas." He opened a desk drawer and tossed her a sack which hit the small side table with an audible clink. Three hundred coins, though small and gold, added up to a nice weight.

She put out her hand and drew the bag toward her. Looking inside she saw enough money to enable her mother to live at her ease for several years. But it made her resentful that it had come so easily.

"You may count it."

"No need."

"You trust me?"

"No, but my mistrust of you has nothing to do with money." She stood up and went toward the door with the purse in her hands.

Wyle felt he should say something else to her, but he realized he had offended her somehow. "Shall I have my carriage put to? After you change, I mean."

"Your carriage?" She turned to face him, her dark hair coiling around her neck, her luscious brown eyes sleepy and vacant. "Why? I am not going anywhere."

"But this was only for the one night. You understood that?"

She stared at him as though he was mad. "I understand nothing at the moment. Who knows, but with a night's sleep I may be able to puzzle it out."

As she exited the room with the same grace that had carried her through the evening, Wyle looked after her, feeling the effervescence of the wine dissipating from his veins. It had felt good to put one over on the relatives. Now they would stop introducing him to every whey-faced miss who entered the *ton*. Now Cousin Isabelle would have to stop thrusting her daughter Sophie at him.

But how could he dislodge the woman? He couldn't have her here with his children in the same house. Though the ways he might use to discourage her could make for an intriguing dalliance. But if he planned anything like that, he would have to send the children to Fair Oaks. And that dratted governess had not arrived yet. What the devil was her name? Mr. Hill had made the arrangements. That he would deal with in the morning. For tonight he must think of a plan to get rid of this harpy without paying her more than he had agreed. He went upstairs to his study in order to struggle with the problem.

Only when he became completely sober hours later did he realize how he had put himself in her power. Hiring an actress for an evening seemed simple enough, but he had announced that they were engaged to no fewer than fifteen people. She could sue him for breach of promise, unless he made her so miserable that she wanted to break the engagement. These theater people. They never knew their place.

She had not always been an actress if her father was indeed Major Greenway. This start probably only happened when her father went missing. And since he had been declared missing and not decreed dead, there would have been no pension for the widow and daughter. On his way to bed he tried her door, just out of curiosity. Bolted. So she had no intention of seducing him. Good. He had no intention of succumbing. He had all night to plan what to do about her.

Chapter Two

Marian turned in bed and thought for a moment she still dreamed. Though she distinctly remembered locking the door and indeed heard someone try it last night, she saw a can of hot water waiting for her and a tray with tea and toast by the bed. Marian guessed she had Susan to thank for this consideration, not Wyle. She slipped her hand under the bank of pillows and found the sack of guineas. Whatever happened now, she had more than earned this much and could leave today knowing that if she went to stay with her mother at the cottage she would not have to work for a year or more.

Her own former governess had been so good as to give shelter to her mother, lend Marian enough money to get to London—and write her a letter of reference, for that matter. She certainly wasn't going to get one from the household which had discharged her after Cousin Cole made a nuisance of himself.

Ceres Macomber had rescued Marian so often in the past it seemed natural to run to her. Asking her mother to share her small cottage was generous, but they could not impose on her forever. Marian was surprised Ceres had heard of such a good situation, but if this position did not work out, Marian must not worry her dearest Ceres again.

How unjust that one night's work had bought them at least a year's security. But the end of that time would come soon enough, so she may as well stay here and try to make peace with Lord Wyle.

She washed up, put on her gray morning dress, and redid her hair into a prim bun. Then she had the tea at a small table in front of the window. It looked out over the stable yard and stables, an extravagance for a London town house. The back area also contained a small rose garden off to one side behind a hedge. If only she got to walk out there before she had to leave. Really, it was unfair of him to judge her inadequate as a governess without even letting her try.

The whole house looked extravagant. As a governess she would not have expected to be so well treated and have a room on the second floor, with jonquil wallpaper and a fireplace, not to mention diaphanous bed hangings. Most governesses were relegated to a cold attic.

But what if he wanted more from her than a governess should supply? On the other hand, Lord Wyle could be mentally unstable. She would do well to keep that in mind. His Aunt Flora had mentioned his wounds. Perhaps his head injury manifested itself in such wild flings. A soldier might be expected to have loose morals, but nothing like what had occurred last night.

Still none of his relatives had rolled their gaze heavenward as though his engagement was one of his starts. In fact, a few of them had greeted her with expressions of relief. She began to wonder who had preceded her here as governess.

She secreted the coins in various compartments in her trunk and portable writing desk, with a dozen in her reticule in case she needed them in a hurry. As soon as she had a chance, she would send a bank draft to her mother. No, not too quickly. Else she would wonder how Marian had come by the money. She would wait a day or two and send a portion, telling her it was a clothing allowance. That should suffice. Amazing how practiced she had become at prevarication now that their survival and her mother's peace of mind depended on it. But having money, real money, seemed such a novelty she realized she enjoyed keeping want from the door more than she should.

After donning a gray shawl and covering her hair with a lace cap, she explored the other door in the room and discovered it led to a dressing room and thence to another bedchamber. So if Wyle had really wanted to get in, he could have. She shook her head. A maid came along the hall with a tea tray and Marian said, "I am the new governess, Miss Greenway. Could you show me the way to the schoolroom?"

The maid stared at her with surprise. "Yes, miss. I am just taking tea there."

They went up a floor and Marian followed the maid into a pleasant room where two children were sitting at a wooden work table, plainly eager for their breakfast. The girl wasn't precisely a child. Marian judged her to be fifteen or sixteen, while the boy was six or seven. Both had the family stature but the son favored his father while Charlotte's face looked more delicate, her eyes a soft and arresting brown and her hair a golden bounty that would mark her as a beauty next spring or the one after. Both children stared at Marian raptly.

"I am Miss Greenway, the governess your father has hired. May I join you?"

The maid put down the tray and left. The girl got up to curtsy and tugged at her brother's sleeve. He slid off his chair and bowed. "I am Charlotte and this is Henry." Charlotte carefully picked up the teapot and began to serve quite properly. "How do you take your tea?"

"Just with milk. Thank you." Marian sat and placed a napkin in her lap. Henry sat again while Charlotte finished pouring, then suffered another glare until he napkined his lap.

"Scone?" Charlotte asked, offering the plate to Marian first, then to Henry.

"Yes, please." She found herself smiling. She had seen children like this at her previous post. The family was wealthy and the children had everything except the attention they craved. They tried so hard to be good, but it got them only the kindness of the servants, including her. And in the end she had to leave them because of her Cousin Cole's interference. She hoped he would not be able to find her in London.

Henry finally shut his mouth and looked nervously from his sister to Marian. "Are you going to stay with us forever?"

"I suppose that is up to you two. Though your father engaged…" She swallowed hard. "Though he hired me, I would not stay if you two dislike me. So I think we should try to get acquainted and find out, don't you?"

"Yes," Charlotte said. "I will start. I know my grammar and sums. I also read Italian and French a little. I had started to do watercolor when Miss Grey left."

Henry had just taken a huge bite of scone and chewed fast so he could talk.

"I'll go next," Marian said. "I've had only one position before this and was sorry to leave." She hesitated as she groped for a truth she could tell. "Children do a have a way of growing up. I can teach history, geography, Latin, if there is a need, French, and a little Spanish. I also play the pianoforte and dabble in watercolor. Perhaps we can explore that art together."

Henry swallowed and cleared his throat. "I am terrible at grammar and sums and I don't see why I should learn French. They are the enemy."

"Father says we need to know our enemies," Charlotte supplied.

Marian smiled. "What do you want to learn, Henry?"

The boy looked startled, as though no one had ever asked him this before. "How to ride and shoot like my father."

"A very admirable ambition. My father is a soldier too, and he taught me to shoot a pistol and ride. I suppose I could teach you if your father allows me."

"Really?" Henry's eyes grew round.

"Where did your father fight?" Charlotte asked.

"In Spain. Lord Wyle seems to remember my father. Has he told you anything about the war?"

"He doesn't like to talk about it," Charlotte whispered, "or about Mother. He is writing his memoirs, but he says when they are done we cannot read them."

"Thank you for warning me. We should respect his wishes. Henry, what do you want to be when you grow up?"

"That's easy. A soldier, an artillery officer."

"An artillery officer needs to know his mathematics. He must calculate the distance to the enemy, the trajectory of his missiles, and how much powder to use. I can teach you that."

"Oh, so there is a use for it?" Henry looked more startled than disappointed.

Marian nodded and caught a fleeting smile from Charlotte which deepened into a conspiratorial grin when their gazes met. At least Henry was honest, and that she could build on.

\*\*\*\*

Wyle nursed a throbbing head in the breakfast parlor, but a cup of strong black coffee had begun to alleviate the pain by the time Frobisher was admitted. Like most officers on leave he did not wear his uniform but civilian clothes, and he had cast off the sling that supported his broken arm during his recuperation.

"Morning, Wyle. Sorry about last night."

Wyle glared at Frobisher, who had been with him at school and was his lieutenant in the Peninsula. When not in battle, Fro's vacuous gaze might lead one to believe there was nothing going on in his head. But he stood Wyle's best friend. The man had already helped himself to a cup of coffee from the sideboard and now loaded a plate with food. His brown hair was tousled and his blue eyes red from drink.

"Join me?"

"Yes, I am famished. Why aren't you eating?"

Wyle sent his friend an accusing look.

"Oh, the actress. I am so sorry." He sawed a chop in two and took an enormous bite, then mumbled, "You should eat something. Bit of a disaster, was it?"

"Not up to a point. But now she won't leave. I half expect her to hold me to the engagement."

Frobisher choked. "What? But I went round this morning and she said she hadn't come, that she felt too tired."

"Well she must have sent a replacement, for an attractive woman appeared last night and charmed everyone and…"

"And what?"

Wyle leaned back in his chair. "I don't know how to describe her, but she seemed to fit in, she seemed to belong. Not nervous, she laughed in all the right places. She made everyone feel at ease. She almost acted like it was all real."

"Must have sent her stand-in." Frobisher chewed another bite as he thought. "Why are you so amazed? She *is* an actress, after all."

"Nobody is that good, and without any coaching."

Frobisher stared at him, knife and fork suspended above his plate. "What do you mean she won't leave?"

"She said she didn't understand the arrangement but that she might by morning. Ten to one if I try to get rid of her she will sue me for breach of promise."

"I hadn't thought of that."

"Neither had I." Wyle downed the rest of his coffee. "I just wanted to get my relatives off my back until I go back to my unit. Do you think you could reason with her?"

"Is she pretty?"

"She's beautiful, really, and not an insipid beauty." Wyle stared out the low window into the rose garden as he pictured Marian. "She has deep brown eyes and glorious long dark hair. She hasn't cropped it like most of these young twits. And her voice—it's soft yet distinct, as though she is sure of herself and her opinions."

"That also I expect of an actress. You sound half in love with her yourself. Are you sure you have no interest?"

"Fro, my children are in the house."

"Oh, right." He finished his meal in deep thought. "Perhaps I can offer her a long-term engagement elsewhere, not marriage but something not quite as dull as staying here."

"Oh, really?" Wyle leaned forward, dropping the front chair legs into the floor.

"No offense, Wyle, but you have become a dull dog. You never go anywhere. You lost your wife years ago. You really should look about you and find someone—for real."

"Now you sound like Aunt Alva."

"So where is the woman now?"

"Probably lounging in bed, plotting."

Frobisher wiped his fingers on his napkin and cast it on the table as he rose. "Wish me luck."

Wyle followed Frobisher upstairs, taking the steps two at a time since he couldn't bend his right knee much. They encountered a maid coming out of the woman's chamber with a tray. "Where is she?" he asked without ceremony.

"In the schoolroom having breakfast with the children."

"What?" Wyle staggered back against the wall, then plunged up the next flight of stairs with Frobisher in his wake. When he threw the door open, Charlotte was pointing at the wall map and Henry sat on the sofa beside a strange woman dressed in a sober gray gown and shawl.

"I thought—I thought…" Wyle stammered.

Frobisher stared at her. "Are you Miss Morton's friend?"

"I do not know a Miss Morton. I am Miss Greenway, the new governess. And you are?"

Into the appalled silence Henry said, "Lieutenant Frobisher."

"Pleased to meet you. Would you gentlemen like to join us? We've ordered another pot of tea."

Wyle felt himself swaying on his feet, for though she looked nothing like the woman he had forced to don a glittering ball gown last night, the voice remained the same—confident, cultured, and calculating.

"No, we don't want any tea," he spat out in despair.

"Wait," she said. "Frobisher? The Frobisher you mentioned last night?" She stared at Wyle. "Perhaps you can shed some light on the events of the evening." Marian stood and picked up a pointer that made Frobisher skirt the sofa warily in his efforts to get a better look at her.

Wyle tried to pull himself together. "I-I did not realize you had arrived, Miss Greenway. May I see you in my study?"

"Yes, of course. I shall be down directly."

As they went back downstairs, Frobisher said, "False alarm. That certainly is a governess. The actress must have left during the night."

When they passed Miss Greenway's room, Wyle, who had always told Frobisher everything, decided to keep this one very embarrassing incident to himself. "Yes, she must have left like Cinderella after the ball."

"And you were worried. There isn't so much as a stray slipper to betray her presence."

****

Twenty minutes later when Marian presented herself in Wyle's study on the second floor, she thought Lord Wyle looked worried. In fact, when he had come into the schoolroom he had looked like a stunned ox. Now, why?

"Miss Green."

"Greenway." Rather than sitting she stood with her hands on the back of a chair facing the desk. Of course this meant that Wyle could not sit either.

"I thought you went by Green to save your family embarrassment."

"No, you misheard me last night."

He looked thoughtful as though replaying the evening in his mind. "It won't work."

She shook her head. "What are you talking about?"

"After last night I cannot allow you to teach my children."

"But you ordered me to pretend to be your fiancée. Now you are blaming me?"

"I thought you were someone else." He turned toward the window rather than face her.

She stared at him wondering if he *had* gone mad. "Who?"

Wyle blew out a defeated breath. "An actress Frobisher hired to play my fiancée."

"What a very dangerous thing to do." Marian folded her arms and walked around the desk so that he had to face her. "What if she refused to break off the engagement? You would have had to buy your way out of it. She might even sue you for breach of promise."

Wyle shut his eyes against the hammering headache. "Yes, yes, but I wasn't thinking very clearly when I agreed."

"I see, foxed. But I begin to wonder if you ever think clearly. And you an artillery officer. So you did not realize I am the new governess when you ordered me to dine with your party?"

He looked at her finally. "You should have corrected

27

my error."

She glared. "I did not know you had made one. At my last position I did indeed dine with the family. At first yours did not seem like an outlandish request, until I put on the dress." She felt her color rise, unable to suppress the remembered embarrassment.

"And then?" He stared at her with that dent between his eyebrows.

"By then I was angry."

"Yes, I got that. But you went through with it."

"Something in me rebels at creating a scene, especially before people who all seem to wish you well. Your relatives accepted me, a total stranger, for your sake. They care about you more than you care for them, obviously. Now why is that?" She was standing by a large globe that would be so much more use in the schoolroom than here, and she rested her hand on it.

"Still, you have served your purpose and you must go."

"But you promised me a position as governess." Marian steeled herself for just one small lie. "I left my old position in expectation of it." Well, that was true. She could hear the tears in her own voice. Those at least she could stop.

"I will pay you a year's salary."

"You already have. I will work for a year without any other pay just to prove myself."

"I can't have my children exposed to…"

"To what? A hard worker, someone who loves books and the arts?" She bit her lip, having run out of arguments.

"But you also know about deceit, about the games people play in society."

"I very lately came from society myself. And yes, I understand their games. It might benefit your children to know about them as well."

"I said I would pay you."

His voice was hard, implacable. She was losing.

"And you don't see the injustice of paying an actress as much for an evening of entertainment as you would pay a poor governess for a year's labor?"

"It's not the money."

"Easy for you to say since you have it to throw away. I have a mother to support."

"But people know you now as my fiancée. How can I present you to them as a governess? They would recognize you."

"You did not, until I spoke. Frobisher still does not realize it."

"It was your voice." He ducked his head again, unable to look at her, she surmised, when he knew her cause was just.

"They will never see me. *You* need never see me." She gestured with her hands. "Besides, I have two faces, one for the children and one I used to wear when I was in society, the one you saw last night. No one need ever see that face again." If only she could convince him of her ability to disappear, he might let her stay.

Wyle looked at her earnest sweet face and knew a wave of regret. How could such a beauty condemn herself to obscurity? Major Greenway had been announced missing after the battle of San Sebastian, the same one in which Wyle had been wounded. Greenway was thought dead until his body was not found. Then there were rumors of desertion or treason. "Just leave me."

"But what about Charlotte and Henry? They asked me if I would stay forever."

"And I suppose you said you would."

"That would be stupid. I said it was up to them. Children need to feel as though they have some control of their world. You have not given them that feeling."

"I will not hear any more. My carriage will be at the door in half an hour. Get into it. It will take you anywhere you wish to go."

"I wish to go back in time four years to when my father was with me and I was happy. Have you enough money to buy that for me?"

There was a soft rustle of fabric and the door clicked. He was expecting her to slam it. He rang and sent for the traveling carriage, then tried to work on his memoirs of the war, but his secretary, Hill, had not arrived from the country yet. When he tried to write with his injured hand he did nothing but create ink blots. Besides, all he could think of was Marian and her problems.

Major Greenway. He had met him more than once. An honorable man and a courageous one. This talk of defection was ridiculous. Greenway's daughter seemed much like him. He should do something for this girl. He would give the coachman an envelope with a bank draft. That could be handed to her when she was far from here. He took some pains over writing it out with what was now a spider scrawl and rang for a servant to carry it to the stable.

He missed his old life. He hated sending messages and having servants dance attendance on him. He missed the informality of Peninsular days. Riding to hounds during the long breaks in the fighting or even riding out to battle had an expectancy to it. Everything was in the future then. He was only thirty-five years old, yet he felt an old man and useless. Hiding behind a charade because he felt too pummeled by life to try to build anything new.

The door opened and he looked up to confront Charlotte's flashing brown eyes and a determined set to her chin he had never seen before. She looked a little like her mother Louisa when she was angry.

"What have you done to Miss Greenway?"

"I dismissed her. It was not well done of her to come running to you."

"She did not. I found her in her room in tears. Why are you sending her away? We like her."

"Because…because she argues with me."

"When you are wrong? If you think to escape that, then brace yourself, Father, for I will always argue with you. You had no reason to dismiss her. She told us about her father the major and her mother in the little cottage. She needs this position. And we need her." Charlotte leaned both hands on the desk and stared at him.

"She was trying to get your sympathy."

His daughter glared at him. "I know real tears when I see them. I have cried enough of them."

Suddenly he looked at Charlotte and realized she was not a child anymore. She had grown up when he wasn't looking, and that stabbed at his heart.

"I know you don't understand about your mother's—about her leaving you."

"Who cares about Mother now? I scarcely knew her. She was never with us. Neither were you. Then Mother went off to Italy without us and died there."

"There was a war on."

"And Miss Grey, all the servants, they kept us in this

house like prisoners. I always dreaded coming to London because we never got to see any of it. Even at Fair Oaks there was no riding, nothing but a sedate walk. Miss Greenway promised to teach us everything. She's not afraid of living like you are."

He stared at her a moment, the passionate look, the determined chin, then heard the carriage in the street. Footsteps on the stairs would be the men coming for her trunks. In a very few moments it would be too late to do anything, and Charlotte...she might hate him. Something flashed in his mind from an encounter with Major Greenway, and he jumped up. A sharp pain bit into his knee but he limped to the door anyway and threw it open into the hall. "Stop! Where are you taking that trunk?"

Miss Greenway, two steps down the stairs already, looked both angry and fearful. She must think he was going to confiscate her wages. "Put it back in Miss Greenway's room. She is staying." He plundered his distraught mind for some reason for this change of heart and realized he need only find an excuse that would convince Charlotte and the servants. "I have agreed to her salary."

He rather enjoyed the way Miss Greenway's delicate brows came together when he had puzzled her. She looked very much as she had the night before when he had dragged her up the stairs.

"Charlotte, go get your pelisse and Henry."

The girl looked stunned. "But where are we going, Father?"

"To see London."

"Yes!" Charlotte shouted as she hiked up her skirts and ran up the stairs.

"What—what has happened, sir?" Marian came up to the landing, looking at him again as though he had indeed lost his reason.

Wyle limped toward her as the footmen shook their heads and replaced the baggage. "I remembered something your father said to me—'Don't let the passage of time decide anything for you. Act even if it may be a mistake. At least it is your mistake.' "

Marian blinked. "I am quite sure he was talking about battle."

"I am not. Ah, here come the children. The carriage is at the door. Where shall we go first?"

She still looked confused, but a smile was breaking upon her lips. "Perhaps an improving museum?"

"No, no," Henry said. "The Tower with the animals."

"The Tower it is, then." Wyle took Marian's arm and they followed the children down the stairs. Those were tears on her lashes, but he thought it had to do with more than herself. How could he have neglected his two children so much? Just because he could not love their mother should not have meant he withheld his love from them.

Chapter Three

Five hours later the expedition returned to the house, the children tired but laughing as they carried their booty to their rooms. Marian had not let Wyle buy her anything but a package of ribbons, but she laid it reverently on her bed and kicked off her slippers. It seemed like a dream to her now, not just his change of heart but how he had acted today. He had seemed happy, or at least determined to fake it extremely well. It made Marian wonder how unhappy he was in the depths of his soul, to have pushed his children away for so long.

His coachman had been surprised by the orders to drive to the Tower, then to the docks where Wyle had haggled expertly and purchased exotic fruits and produce. Charlotte now had two lovebirds in a wicker cage. Fortunately there had been no monkeys for sale, but Henry had not given up the idea.

They had lunched and had ices at a hotel, then driven up Oxford Street, stopping at any shop that took their fancy. Since it had drizzled for an hour while they were driving around the parks no one questioned why Lord Wyle had chosen his covered traveling carriage for an expedition around the city. No one questioned him at all, though Marian noted that she was not the only one who stared at him as though he had run mad.

She sighed and glanced at her reticule. She extracted the envelope the coachman had handed her on their return and broke the seal to discover a check for five hundred pounds. What was she to make of that?

The maid who had been attending to her needs arrived, breathless, to ask if she would join Lord Wyle for dinner later that evening.

Marian looked so dubious the girl rushed ahead with her message.

"And if it pleases you, I am to become your personal maid."

That meant he wanted her to stay. "Would that please you, Susan?"

"Oh, yes. Would you like me to bring hot water?"

"Yes, I would like a bath very much."

When she was gone, Marian reflected that a promotion from upstairs maid to personal maid, even of a governess, might double the girl's wages. No matter how poor she felt, she must remember that there were many thousands of hardworking people far worse off than she was. And even they had to keep up appearances.

Dining with Wyle? There was much she needed to say to him, but not over dinner. Still, he had been so good to the children today she wanted to thank him. Besides, who would know they dined alone?

Several hours later, she donned her lavender dress, placed an elegant lace cap on her head, and went to the drawing room with her lips pressed tightly together. When she entered, Wyle heaved himself up from the chair where he had been brooding and came to inspect her.

"Which face are you wearing tonight?" His gaze fastened on her cap.

"The governess one, of course. That is what I promised."

"Does that mean you will not smile at me at all?"

She sat down and let him pour her a sherry. "How could I withhold that slight approval when you have made your children so happy today?"

"Was it unfair of me to offer them a diet of sweets today when I have so long denied them a meal of affection?" He seated himself across from her and reached for his wine glass.

"I regarded it as a promise of more of your attention in future." She thought he choked a little on his wine. "And I assure you, so do they."

"The war is over, or nearly so. I do intend to spend more time with them in future."

"Speaking of the future, what am I to make of that envelope the coachman gave me?"

"Oh, that. Your first year's salary, of course, unless you think you are worth more."

"That is more than satisfactory, so long as you are hiring only a governess."

He looked surprised or feigned it very well, then smiled.

"Of course. What did you think I meant by it?"

"I was not sure, sir. That is why I asked. Would you like me to play for you until dinner?" The vast room seemed empty with only the two of them.

"You play the pianoforte well."

"Yes, that was in my credentials, if you recall."

His eyebrows got that mark of concentration between them.

"You do recall that, or did you not read them?"

He looked down. "My secretary takes care of such matters for me."

"I see. You did not read them."

"No." He faced her with the hint of a smile.

"But not the harp."

"What?"

She glanced toward the imposing instrument with some unease. It sat in the corner of the room near the piano, some music stands, and half a dozen chairs. She knew that musical entertainments were once the fashion in this home and hoped he had no such aspirations for the future.

"That was my wife's. It was the only thing she knew how to do."

"She produced two lovely children with you. You have to give her credit for that."

For a moment his brow turned as black as thunder, then it eased into that now familiar dent between his brows. "A reluctant contribution to our marriage. She did not want children by me. I see by your face that surprises you."

"I should not assume all women want children, though it does seem to be expected of us."

"Do you?"

She smiled tightly, not her alluring society smile but her prim governess smile. "It takes more than wanting. There must be provision. I can barely take care of my mother. I would be ill-equipped to have children. Besides, I am not married and am not likely to be." She said this to let him know that she really only wanted to be the governess, that the sham engagement was just that, a fiction.

"As to that, it takes more than money to raise children, as I have proven."

"But it is not too late. Henry is young. Charlotte is understanding."

Wyle gave a harsh laugh and tossed off the rest of his wine. "And thank God for that. Do you know why I called you back today?"

"As with most things you do, I am in the dark. You didn't suffer…"

He shot her a frank look. "What? An attack of conscience?"

"I was going to say a loss of reason from your head wound."

Wyle coughed. "No, at least not that I recall."

"Then from your quoting of my father, I lay your behavior down to the caprices of a soldier used to taking action even if it is risky."

His smile seemed pained. "I called you back because dutiful, understanding Charlotte burst into my office and told me I was making a huge mistake for which she would never forgive me. That she and Henry were virtual prisoners both here and at Fair Oaks. It made me realize how ill done it was of me to leave them in the charge of servants while I went off to war."

"Then you mean to sell out and remain with them?"

"It is unlikely I will be called back to duty. But if I am, I trust I can leave them in your care."

"But, and I point this out as a matter of form, I am a servant."

"Oh, no."

He rested his head on his fist and stared at her with that penetrating gaze that she imagined would make a subaltern check for smudges on his uniform. She refused to glance at her lavender dress.

Then he shook his head slowly. "I do not know what you are, Miss Greenway, but you are no servant."

She placed her glass carefully in the side table.

"Would you like me to play for you until dinner?"

"You are the only person I know who retreats from an untenable position to the center of focus. Yes, I would like it of all things."

When her fingers touched the keys, he realized he was not to be treated to light ballads. The chords of the music echoed off the oak paneling as though they were words trying to say something very significant to him if only he understood the language. Wyle had seated himself close to the piano prepared to be amused. He was not prepared to be stunned, to be touched. If only he had met this woman years ago when he was looking for a wife. But she would have been, what? Five years old? Still, he had let his well-meaning relatives stampede him into marriage.

But then he thought of Charlotte and Henry. It did not do to regret your life, for to turn back the clock would lose him all the good things as well as Louisa's tantrums, her homesickness and constant demands to be able to go to Paris in spite of the war. He thought she had marred his life forever, but just at this moment, listening to the soft fall of Marian's fingers on the keys, he could not even remember what Louisa looked like.

Marian played until Trumby opened the door to announce dinner, but Wyle would far rather have listened to her than sit down to even the best of meals. On their way into the dining room he asked, "Will you play something else after dinner?"

"Yes, but I thought you might like to have the children come down for tea."

"Of course. They would like your playing too. You will teach Charlotte the pianoforte?"

"She is eager to learn."

Wyle seated her in the first chair to the left of his position at the head of the table. While they waited for servants to lay slices of capon and portions of the other removes on their plates, he could see Marian working up to a subject. It was the firmness of her mouth that gave her away. She compressed her lips when she was planning to say something.

She took a sip of wine and picked up her cutlery. "I was just thinking how nice it would be to have Charlotte dine with us. She could learn so much. I'm not sure why children are relegated to the schoolroom when dinner could be a time of profitable instruction."

He knew why he would rather not have Charlotte present, but it had nothing to do with his daughter. He also realized too late why Marian would like Charlotte here. Even the rougher manners of the Peninsula would not have provided for a single genteel lady to dine alone with an eligible male. The presence of the servants, though they seemed overly attentive and scarcely left them alone for a moment, meant nothing for her reputation. Why had he not thought of it before?

He took a delaying sip of wine, wondering if it was too late to send for Charlotte tonight and was not surprised to hear someone at the door. Frobisher let himself into the dining room, drawing a stony stare from the butler.

"Am I interrupting anything?" Frobisher asked, staring in some confusion at Marian.

"Would it matter if you were?" Wyle countered.

Marian chuckled at Wyle's comment, but she sounded relieved. True, Frobisher added nothing to the situation as a chaperon. Possibly he made the evening worse. But to deny him a place at the table now would be ill-advised since he could not trust what Fro might say when in his cups. Tomorrow it would definitely have to be Charlotte.

Trumby came to attention. "Shall I set another place, sir?"

"No, let him eat off the cloth."

The butler glared at Wyle and produced another place setting from the cupboard. He then served Frobisher and got a rousing thanks in return. Trumby then left them until the second course was needed.

"Are you going out tonight, Wyle?"

"No, I plan to stay in and listen to Miss Greenway while she plays for the children."

"How dull."

Marian choked.

"The staying-in part," Frobisher amended. "Not your playing."

"You have not heard me play, Mr. Frobisher. How can you judge?"

The man took too large a gulp of wine and had trouble getting it down. "How can a music recital hold a candle to the opera?"

Marian smiled ever so slightly. It was in fact an admonishing smile. "If by the opera you mean ogling the dancers in the ballet number, then no, I suppose I would not shine next to them."

"You are making me sound like a toad," he accused.

Wyle's lips curled into a patient smile. "You are doing that yourself, Frobisher. You may dine with us and stay for the evening, but you will watch your mouth around my children."

"Wyle, you are becoming positively staid."

"And about time. As Miss Greenway has reminded

me, Charlotte and Henry have been without me enough of their lives."

"I thought you meant to go back into action as soon as your leg mended."

"News from the front is that the French are headed back across the Pyrenees. The war may soon be over."

"You cannot leave the army. What about your friends?"

Wyle glared at him. "What about all my relatives?"

"You can dodge them much better in Europe than in England."

"The trick is to seem to do what they want so they stop interfering."

"Yes, I thought that fake engagement was one of my more brilliant ideas."

Marian stared at him. "So it was your idea. I might have known."

"Now see here—just a moment. Why has Wyle told you about our plan?"

Wyle sighed and put down his glass. "Because I assumed Miss Greenway was the actress you hired."

"What? But how could you mistake a respectable governess for an actress? Have you taken leave of your senses?"

Marian failed to suppress a small snort of laughter.

Wyle winced. "Apparently."

She turned to the lieutenant. "What were you thinking, Frobisher, by suggesting such a scheme? As soon as he breaks the engagement he will be right back where he started, with the aunts interfering."

"Yes, but now he has you."

"What is that supposed to mean?" she demanded.

"To governess the children, I mean."

She shook her head. "That is not what you were thinking."

"What am I supposed to think, the two of you here dining *en famille*, alone?" Frobisher waggled his brown eyebrows up and down, and Wyle laughed.

Marian thought Wyle was three parts drunk and was embarrassed to have her indiscretion pointed out to her. If Wyle did not know it was improper for her to dine alone with him, then she did, which is why she was going to insist on Charlotte joining them.

"Well, whatever it was, put it out of your mind," she said.

Wyle had been thinking during this lively exchange and finally interrupted.

"He's right."

"What?" Marian demanded.

"It does not look well for us to be dining alone."

"Very well," Marian said as she rose to her feet. "I will retire to the schoolroom."

Wyle grabbed her hand to halt her flight, his touch gentle yet compelling. "Sit down, please. We have Frobisher for propriety tonight."

"Frobisher?" she choked out but she did sit again.

"And tomorrow night we will have Charlotte and Henry dining with us."

"We will?" Marian asked.

"Yes, it is the perfect solution."

Frobisher stared at his friend. "You have some strange ideas about perfection."

"But at least they are my ideas, not someone else's put to me when I was in my cups and generally a wreck."

"You were never like this during the war." Frobisher went to the sideboard to replenish the wine in his glass.

"The war is over for me."

"Tell me you won't dig out that uniform and have your charger shod as soon as we are engaged again." He sat back down and plunged into his meal.

"I tell you I won't. Between the children and Fair Oaks, I have enough to handle."

Frobisher grumbled through the rest of the meal, but he did stay. When Marian withdrew to the drawing room to arrange music, Wyle rang and sent for the children, causing his butler's eyebrows to get even more exercise.

Frobisher glared at Wyle. "What are you playing at?"

"What do you mean?" Wyle poured port into two glasses and handed one to his friend. Usually this would have silenced Fro, but the man simply sniffed the liquor.

"You know what I mean. Are you planning to turn Miss Greenway into a lightskirt?"

"Certainly not. In this case, my intentions are honorable."

"They had better be. If I mistake not, she has a father in the cavalry who will call you out if they are otherwise."

"Unfortunately, it appears Major Greenway is either dead or captured."

"Ah, so this is one of your charitable impulses." Frobisher leaned back in his chair with satisfaction. "You are too soft-hearted, Wyle. Everyone knows that."

"That is how it started out, but I begin to see the wisdom of Aunt Alva's views."

Fro choked on the sip he had finally taken. "Your Aunt Alva, the one you are always dodging?"

"She says I need to get married again and I intend to. Miss Greenway just doesn't know it yet."

"And what makes you think your attentions will be welcome? She seems a frosty woman, to me."

"She is already invested in the welfare of my children. If I don't make any fantastic blunders she might also come to like me."

"But you can't have it both ways. She can't be your children's governess *and* your fiancée."

"Why not?"

Frobisher stared at him. "It will look like you seduced her."

"But I cannot send her away now. The children need her."

"Then you can never marry her."

Wyle downed the rest of his port in one incautious gulp and immediately felt dizzy. Why did he argue with Fro? He never won. But was his friend right in this case? Perhaps he should consult Aunt Alva, but the mere thought gave him such a shudder. He stood and invited Frobisher to the recital. To his surprise, the man agreed.

Charlotte looked very grown up and Henry sleepy but they sat through one of Miss Greenway's sonatas with rapt attention. When the tea tray arrived, Wyle glanced at Marian but she said, "Charlotte, you serve tea so prettily. Would you like to do it tonight?"

"I-I shall try not to spill any."

"Not on your brother or Miss Greenway, at any rate," Wyle joked. "But if you want to dump some on Frobisher or me, that is completely fine."

Charlotte laughed and it was like a bell tinkling. He was glad he'd hit on the right comment to put her at her ease. Wyle wondered how he could have let so many years pass without appreciating this child. Henry watched everything, so wide-eyed he almost forgot to eat his cake.

As soon as he had swallowed his tea, Frobisher left.

"How did I do?" Charlotte asked.

Marian smiled at Wyle and he said, "Perfect."

She was right to prompt him. Charlotte needed to hear the word from his lips, not hers. How odd. Marian Greenway had been in the house only a day and everything seemed completely changed. How was this possible?

He went to bed speculating on some hard truths. He wasn't getting any younger. He was engaged to this woman, as far as his relatives knew. All he had to do was put off breaking up with her. If she grew used to the idea of being engaged to him, perhaps she might agree to marry him.

And to think that last night he had been devising ways to get rid of her. Her acerbic comments had a certain calming effect on him and everyone else. And those eyes, like deep pools you could lose your soul in.

When she was not pretending to be prim, her lips pouted lushly and made him want to kiss her troubles away and fold her in his arms forever.

No matter how she tried to hide her beauty behind that cold stare, she failed.

Marian Greenway was a passionate, loving woman, and no lace cap could disguise her spirit.

Chapter Four

As they breakfasted in the schoolroom, Marian contemplated what had happened with Wyle the day before. Now both the children would have Lord Wyle's attention, though Henry needed it even more than Charlotte right now. But she wondered if Wyle would be up to the plans she had made for today. The children talked of nothing but the day before.

"Will we get to come down again tonight?" Charlotte asked.

"You are to dine with us tonight, both of you."

Henry choked on his muffin. "Both of us? Are you sure? Trumby threatened to cut my head off the last time, when I broke a plate."

"Yes, and every night unless your father invites company, and then I shall not dine with him either. Finish up. We have a big day ahead of us. Here is our schedule."

They put their heads together over the sheet of paper.

"A riding lesson, the first thing? Yippee!" Henry's joy was wonderful to behold.

"Well, I hope so. First, we have to convince your father. He does have four riding horses, doesn't he?"

"He must have a dozen horses," Henry chimed.

"Half of those are carriage horses," Charlotte said. "But will he let us?"

"I have sent word to the stable to saddle three hacks

for eight o'clock. If we just pretend this is normal, perhaps he will too."

From one of Louisa's old trunks they unearthed a red riding habit that more or less fitted Charlotte. It would do until they could have one made for her. Marian wore her newer habit, the dark green one in the same color as a rifleman's uniform.

At precisely eight, Marian and Charlotte descended the stairs in riding dress. Henry jumped down every other step until Marian reminded him that if he strained an ankle he would not get to ride.

To her surprise and delight there were five horses saddled and Wyle was standing at the head of one of them, a tall, hard-muscled gray. In her mind she assigned the sleepy hack to Henry, the sleek mare to Charlotte, and the restless chestnut to herself. She had not wanted to ask about Wyle's leg, whether it prevented him riding. She preferred to leave the option open to him to come if he was able. So not teaching the children up until now had been because of lack of time rather than of ability? Or perhaps lack of thought.

As he lifted her into the saddle of the chestnut, he said between gritted teeth, "I would appreciate a little warning when you plan an expedition."

"It's not an expedition. It's a lesson, and I plan on taking the children riding every morning it does not rain. Didn't you read the schedule I left on the desk in your study?"

He stared at her, his mouth agape, and finally she saw a resemblance to Henry.

"I must have mislaid it," he finally said. "I only knew what you planned because my head groom does consult with me, unlike some of my employees."

By now both Henry and Charlotte were mounted on exactly the horses she would have chosen for them. The gray brute Wyle mounted was definitely a leader. The chestnut mare under her she thought had some fire in her, but she did not intend to let her show it today. It would not impress either Wyle or his children if she got herself thrown.

"In so far as possible, I think we should walk the horses today. Do you agree, Lord Wyle?"

"Oh, through the streets, yes. Once we get to the park, we'll see."

She noticed him switching the reins about in his hands and realized that the scar that ran between the thumb and forefinger on his right hand indicated an injury that would have been career-ending for a cavalry man. Finally, he put the reins for the curb bit in his strong left hand and the snaffle reins in his right. She recalled all her father's war horses had been double-bitted like this with one set of reins for braking and one for steering. It took courage to ride a hard-mouthed army horse with only one sound hand.

He and Miss Greenway led the way, and a groom rode after the children, whose mounts followed side by side. Wyle thought he should make a push to assert himself about the riding lessons. He wanted his children to ride well so they could tour the estate, not just for show in Hyde Park. "Miss Greenway, I should be able to teach my own children how to ride."

"Well, that is what I was hoping, but I feared you might not have time, what with writing your memoirs."

"Of course I have time. I didn't even know they were interested."

She turned her head and looked at him expectantly.

He looked embarrassed. "And yes, I should have known they wanted this."

"They are interested in a great many things. You have intelligent children. You should get to know them better."

Wyle nodded. Intelligent children, as opposed to him who was not so intelligent. Well, it was a just slur and delivered with such a deft hand that not even the groom got it. He had neglected his children. Why was that? As they plodded sedately over the cobblestones, he decided they had always reminded him of their mother, and he had such bitter memories of her he had let it poison his relationship with them. All that seemed magically swept away now. He felt he could see clearly for the first time in years.

Wyle cleared his throat. "I suggest that Henry ride beside me and Charlotte next to you, since a sidesaddle creates its own problems."

"A good idea. She asked me why she needs a riding crop and Henry does not."

"And you told her so that he doesn't flog the beast into a runaway?"

Marian laughed. "Of course not. I told her so she can give the horse a signal on the right side since she has no heel or knee there."

"Oh. I had never thought about it very much." What a mistake to say so.

"I'm sure there are any number of things you have not thought of. That is why I am here." She did not say this in a superior way but with the hint of a smile as though she was jesting with him.

"Indeed. You almost sound as though you resent having to ride sidesaddle."

"No, it is a challenge, and I do like a challenge. Women have to be better riders than men and they take more risks. I bet you never thought of that, either."

"No, you shall have to make me a list of things I've never thought of and leave it on my desk as you did the curriculum. That should occupy all your spare time." Wyle glanced back at the children, and Charlotte looked worried. Then he realized she must remember some of the arguments he'd had with her mother, so he smiled at her and got an answering smile in return. Was that all it took to set her mind at rest, a smile? And what with his wounds he probably had denied the children even that for many months.

"We made it to the park," Henry said. "Can we trot now?"

"*May* we trot," Marian corrected. "And that is up to your father."

Wyle was glad she was going to let him decide something, but suddenly he felt protective of these two children he hardly knew. He scrutinized Henry's stirrups and got off to make some adjustments. Then he made them walk the horses and do turns on the grass so they could practice steering before they got back on the pathway.

It was many minutes before he said, "trot" and then he poured forth a bunch of warnings about not letting the horse get the bit, none of which Henry paid the least heed to. Henry let his horse jog and then got white in the face when it loosened to a gallop. "Tug, Henry, tug and release," Wyle said as he matched his gray's stride to the hack. "Tug and release and say, 'Whoa.' You can stop him yourself."

Finally the hack got the idea he could not take

advantage of the boy the way he had planned and slowed to a trot.

"Good job, Henry. You've got it. Make the horse do what you intend and he won't take charge."

"Yes, Father. Did I do well?"

The look the boy sent him was so hopeful it melted Wyle's heart. "You did very well. Now turn in a circle left and let the ladies get ahead of us. I want to see how Charlotte is doing."

With Wyle's mount, Warlock, making a wider circle to the left, the hack had no choice but to obey Henry's guidance and fall in behind Marian and Charlotte. The groom, Hoby, rode out ahead now, probably still worried they might have a runaway. But Marian was a conservative rider, very proper and straight-backed in her posting, and Charlotte was doing a good job of imitating her. There was a constant stream of conversation between them and much laughter. *If only their mother had been a tenth the woman that Marian is.*

When they had made the circuit of the park, Wyle thought he would have no reservation about allowing Charlotte to ride with Marian and a groom. But he wanted to keep Henry under his wing for a while if he could. *If he could?* Of course he could if he chose. Why was he feeling like drawing back from them again? It was that old feeling he had always had between battles, that he should be doing something else, be somewhere else.

But this was where he needed to be, he argued with himself. This was his job here in England, no matter what happened with the army. This was more important than war. He just had to remind himself that he deserved a life even though his errant wife had not thought so.

Their last violent scene came to mind. Henry had been three and Louisa was still refusing him her bed. "You are away for years and only come back to get me pregnant," she accused. "I cannot take another child. I want to go to Italy for my health." And so she had gone, with her cousin. And he had never seen her again. Thank God she had not taken the children. How awful if she had taken them on to Europe with her and they had been trapped there with her during the war. Word had come back about her affair with a French count. Wyle had written asking her to come home, but she had refused and demanded that he send Charlotte to her. *Never! Everything she writes to me is part of a huge deception.*

When the party got back to the house, he declared they would breakfast together. Not the paltry tea and cakes they served in the schoolroom, but ham and bacon. A man's breakfast. Henry needed to talk about his success, and so did Charlotte. As he and his son loaded their plates and sat, his daughter and Marian were discussing the color of Charlotte's proposed riding habit. She wanted a green one like Marian's. Suddenly it occurred to him that Charlotte had been wearing Louisa's, and oddly that did not make him sad. He chuckled as he put milk in his coffee.

"What is so humorous, sir?" Marian asked.

"Rather than discussing the rival points of the horses, you will turn this into a fashion show."

"But, Father, I do need a new riding outfit; the jacket is too tight on this one."

"And you shall have one. Order a dozen, if you like. But I think you need a more spirited mount, as well. I shall send to Fair Oaks. There is a mare there I have in mind for you."

"What about me?" Henry pleaded.

"I think it will be harder to find just the right horse for you, Henry. You might have to try a few before I am satisfied."

"Can we— *May* we ride again tomorrow?" Henry asked.

"Yes, unless it rains." He glanced at Marian and won a smile of approval from her. Not her prim governess smile but her genuine lush smile. Why was that so important to him now? She was wrong about being able to keep her real face hidden forever. Like a fairy tale heroine, her beauty would shine through in spite of her station.

As soon as they had eaten, the children went to the schoolroom to get ready for lessons. Marian hesitated outside the breakfast parlor.

"I am so glad you decided to accompany us."

"So am I," he agreed.

"And that you are taking an interest in their education."

"Of course. Why do you say that?"

She had started up the steps but spun to look at him, looping up the tail of her habit as though it were a queenly train. "Although I am a crack shot, I thought the servants might take it amiss if I started loading pistols in the rose garden."

"What?" He staggered into the wall.

"Look at the curriculum," her quiet voice instructed as she disappeared up the stairs.

He hastened to his study on the next floor and found her list. Henry wanted to learn to shoot. Wonderful! He could just see himself taking a seven-year-old to Manton's. He would be a laughingstock. But if it came to that, he did not really care. He found himself chuckling over their ambitions but with a stab to his now-vulnerable heart. He'd had no idea Henry wanted to be a soldier, that the boy worshiped him.

Perhaps he could devise some substitute for the shooting so that he could save gunfire for their return to Fair Oaks. Miss Greenway would accompany them, of course, and...

A peremptory rap at the door interrupted his thoughts.

The butler opened it without Wyle's permission and announced Lady Ridgeway.

"Glad to see you are up and working, unlike your lazy cousin."

"Good morning, Aunt Alva. What brings you out so early?"

"Plans. We must make plans." She plumped down on the chair in front of his desk before he could even rise.

"Plans for what?"

"Your wedding, of course."

"Oh, well, there is plenty of time for that. Besides, Miss Green...way will want to take care of those. She'll need her trousseau."

"And where will you take her for your wedding tour?"

"Why to Fair Oaks, of course."

"How paltry." Alva glanced around the study as though mentally redecorating it.

"She has never seen it. She will be delighted. Besides, there is a war on. I can hardly take her to Europe."

"Did you even consult her?"

"We have not had leisure to discuss that as yet."

"Well, give me her direction. Someone must make a start." Alva reached for his pen and he snatched it away.

"I will not. You will worry the poor girl to death."

"I can find out where she is staying if you will not tell me."

"Then do so."

Wyle chuckled as his aunt left in a huff. Now that he thought about it, most of the pressure for him to marry again had come from her. Why was it so important that he be attached? If anything was to happen to him, he now had a son to take his place. And if anything was to happen to Henry, well, Morris Armstead would be next in line. But that should not matter to Alva, since her son Edward was ineligible. Now, why did she care if he married or not?

Chapter Five

The morning lessons had gone so well Marian found the need to visit a shop to purchase more books so she could stay ahead of Charlotte. The children had left the luncheon table for a session of French translation when Marian mentioned her need to Lord Wyle. Before she could stop him, he called for the team and she found herself being driven by Lord Wyle to Hatchett's, this time in a phaeton.

"We should have brought the children. They might find something there."

"I see by your schedule that this is study time. We have an hour or so for you to have a rest from them."

"But we agreed I was to keep a low profile. I should have taken a hackney to the bookshop." She tried to shield her face from passing traffic with the umbrella she had brought to fend off rain.

"Why, when I can take you there in comfort? Besides, no one will see us who did not have a chance to ogle us this morning in the park."

"You are probably wondering why I did not voice some concern then."

"No, I wasn't, but I feel sure you will tell me." His smirk showed up the dents beside his mouth.

"It was so wonderful to see the children laughing and having fun with you. Not for the world would I have cut short that expedition, and I did wear a veil over my riding hat. Besides, it was very early."

"But you were not wearing a veil the day before."

"I did not think of it. I was stunned by your transformation. Did you notice anyone you knew?"

"At the Tower? Not likely, and we were in a closed carriage. If any acquaintance did see me, they might think you my Aunt Alva."

"It was worth the risk to entertain them so much."

"It was wonderful, wasn't it? I do not recall ever doing anything like it."

She smiled at him. "Then I am sorry for you."

"I am sorry for me. I have missed so much. Thanks to you, I see the error of my ways. Shall I go in with you? Reed can walk the horses."

"It might be better if I went alone."

"Very well. I have a few errands of my own to take care of. I shall return for you in, say, an hour."

"Yes, thank you."

Marian tried to keep her mind on her purchases, but she kept thinking of Wyle and how different he looked with the children than he had that first night. She kept reminding herself he had been half drunk when they had met. That was why he'd had that dangerous gleam in his eyes, why he had acted so impulsively, and why he had been able to tempt her to be jubilantly indiscreet.

Thank goodness that was over and she could recede into the background, go back to being Miss Greenway again, with the face of a sober governess. Truth to tell, she treasured that one night in her dreams, that brief return to the limelight, where she was poised and witty, where everyone laughed at whatever she said, where Wyle eyed her with longing. He had done that. If her memory served her, that could not have been an act. He had desired her that night. Fortunately, that was past. She could not accomplish her present task if he still harbored any of those feelings for her.

That was a lowering thought, that his attraction to her had come from a bottle. He was a complex man, but she thought she could help him as she educated Charlotte and Henry. Only if she kept her head, only if she wore this sober face.

She was at the counter paying for her purchase when she saw someone familiar. It was one of the relatives from Wyle's party. Isabelle looked her up and down, but Marian kept her eyes resolutely on the clerk. Though Isabelle had a puzzled expression when Marian took her package, the woman did not attempt to speak with her.

It worked. The demure fawn dress and poke bonnet pressed her into the background of life. All she had to do was not make eye contact. A governess or other servant was almost invisible in this world. No one bothered with them. She felt a sense of pride in having pulled that off. Precisely one hour after he had left her, Wyle returned and got down to take her bundle and help her up, though it was completely unnecessary.

"You will give me the bill for those."

"Yes, of course. We should be home in plenty of time for the art lesson. Henry seemed interested, so we shall include him. But he does not want to learn the pianoforte."

"Oh, I have an idea there. Fencing takes much more skill than shooting. I had a notion to give him lessons in the ballroom."

"And as opposed to target practice, it is also nearly silent."

"Precisely, unless we topple a vase or something.

You approve?"

"Yes, I am sure our scales and playing will cover the noise of any breakage."

"I love the way you say things like that as though they are no surprise."

"Are you accusing me of being witty?"

"Yes. You said you had two ways of being, two faces you called it, but you are yourself under those sober clothes."

Marian looked at him, and there was something in his eyes that was more than amusement. Not a dangerous glint but some small fire. This could be a problem.

"Where are we going now? This isn't the way home."

"An airing around the park will take no more than twenty minutes, and I do not want you toiling endlessly."

"But someone might see us."

"Then put on your Mary Green face and smile. No one will think it odd that I take my betrothed for a drive."

When he said things like that, as though he was maintaining the illusion of the engagement, she did not know how to take him. So she glared at him, but it *was* refreshing to drive about the park. She glanced at his hands to find he held both left reins in his left hand and had the right reins of both horses twined through the fingers of his right hand. She supposed the phaeton team knew their business and would not bolt. Still he took a risk, but she would be the last to fuss over his accommodations to civilian life. As an artillery officer, he probably didn't need to use his hands much. She had to keep reminding herself he'd only said he was going to quit soldiering, just as her father had promised to retire. But war was intoxicating to men. Perhaps they were all a little mad in that respect.

**** 

Wyle was making notes in his study, praying for the return of Hill, when a small knock came at the door.

"Come," Wyle commanded.

Charlotte entered carrying a large rough piece of paper stock, followed by Henry with a grubbier sheet of paper. "Look what I did?"

Wyle stood up and took the still damp work from her. "Why, it's the rose garden at Fair Oaks."

"You recognize it?"

"Of course. We will have it framed."

"No, it's not good enough for that. I want to keep it in my room to compare as I progress."

"Well, Henry, how did you do?"

Henry displayed a pencil sketch of a horse.

"It's Warlock. A very good rendering."

"His back is too long and his feet need work, but you did know it was him."

Marian slid into the room behind the children. "We released Henry to sketch in the stable. I think he has a knack for animal studies."

"After he overturned the brush pot," Charlotte said. "He does not have a knack for paints."

Wyle laughed. "Well done, both of you. Now we have time for music practice and fencing before dinner."

While Charlotte practiced scales in the drawing room, Marian sorted music and peeked into the disused ballroom to see Wyle and Henry shuffling back and forth in their stockinged feet on the polished wood floor, using sticks rather than rapiers. Good choice until Wyle could find capped jousting foils and padded vests. Just as she was about to withdraw, the stick slid out of Wyle's right hand and took down a vase with a crash that echoed off the walls.

"Oh, no!" Henry said.

"It was ugly anyway." Wyle added, "Switch hands now."

He wasn't as skilled with his left hand, but he could hang onto his fake weapon. Suddenly Marian realized how very dangerous it would be for Wyle to stay in the army. Not only did his limp impede him, but if it came to hand-to-hand combat, he would be ill-equipped to defend himself. Yet, if she read him right, the possibility of personal danger would never dissuade him from going back to war if the situation was compelling enough. After an hour, Henry and Wyle came into the music room, still breathing hard, and Charlotte stopped playing.

Henry smiled. "What's next? I don't want anything to do with music."

"When Mr. Hill returns, we tackle estate accounts."

"Oh."

Wyle noted Henry's face held resignation rather than the resistance he expected.

"That is something Charlotte should study as well," Marian said. "A woman never knows when she is going to be left in charge of a whole estate."

"You are right," Wyle agreed. "Now, shall we all change for dinner so we can practice our company manners?"

Wyle was glad they had pushed the dinner hour earlier so he would have a longer evening with the children. As he changed into evening dress with the help of his valet, Wyle wondered if that's what had happened to Marian. Had she been left in charge of her father's estate and failed? Had she lost the estate, or was this position a desperate bid to save it still? Perhaps his man of business could find out for him. Or he could just ask Marian. But somehow he thought his interference in that matter would be unwelcome. She was an independent sort and might prefer to save the place by her own hard work rather than have him rescue her.

Chapter Six

Marian told herself the gown she had chosen, a dimity with capped sleeves and lace, was appropriate for a governess, but in her heart she knew she wore the dress for him. When Marian arrived in the drawing room, a tall young man was standing with his back to the street window. He had dark hair and a ready smile for her. Wyle stood to introduce him. "Miss Greenway, may I present Mr. Hill?"

"So happy to meet the Mr. Hill who hired me."

"So happy that all has worked out to everyone's satisfaction," Hill replied, taking her hand.

Wyle clapped him on the back. "I suppose we should call you Reverend Louis Hill, now that you have been ordained."

"I'm glad you understood how important it was that I go home first to tell my parents."

Wyle smiled and told Marian, "Not everyone can care for aged parents and make it through Oxford at the same time. Our fresh reverend will take over for his father at Fair Oaks vicarage when he retires. But for now he is my devoted scribe."

"And very glad for the chance to work on your memoirs, sir."

"Actually, Hill is writing them. I'm just jogging my memory. If the book is ever complete, it will be more to his credit than mine."

"You are too modest, sir."

"I am too honest."

"So I hear the ruffians are coming to practice spoons and forks?" Hill asked nervously.

Marian realized Hill must have been briefed by Trumby. If he had the ear of the staff he would be a good ally for her.

Wyle smiled. "Soon, I hope, though Henry is probably still struggling with his cravat. He won't learn how to tie it if I do it for him every time."

The butler opened the door and ushered the children in. "I have set a place for Lieutenant Frobisher just in case, sir."

Wyle stared at the presumption, then shrugged. "Probably a good idea."

Dinner that evening was a raucous affair uninterrupted by Frobisher or any other caller. Hill was a natural wit and Charlotte well-practiced in guessing his jokes and riposting. Wyle would have little to blush for when she was presented to the *ton*. Marian also thought there was an attraction there, at least a regard. And if that was so, she hoped Wyle had the good sense not to trample it. Many women had done well by marrying a man of the cloth. At least such men were unlikely to take ship for Spain and get themselves shot.

Marian had not laughed so much in years, not since her come-out season. Mother had been proud of her—until she'd refused the best offer that was likely to come to the daughter of a military man, even though her mother was Lady Elizabeth Parkening in her own right. It was from another soldier, and though Marian did not dislike Colonel Pike, she could not bear the thought of waiting at home for letters, wondering if he was dead or alive. Better never to marry than to endure such suspense. If you let yourself love a soldier, it hurt all the more when you lost him.

She recalled her mother's confession, that she had been afraid to fall in love with Marian's father because she always feared she would lose him. Now Marian had learned from Flora it had been a love match.

Finally she said, "It is time for the ladies to retire from the table, but if you two gentleman mean to linger over the port, I think Henry should come with us and study."

Hill laid his napkin on the table. "I have to unpack, but I will join you all in the drawing room in a bit."

"Well, if everyone is going to work, I might as well quit the dining room rather than languish here alone," Wyle said. They all left on their appointed tasks, and he walked with Marian into the hall. "Is there anything else on the agenda for tonight?"

"I thought perhaps a dancing lesson. Now that we have Reverend Hill, we can make use of him for that while I play and you..." She stopped herself when she realized she was inferring he could not dance.

He arched an eyebrow. "Criticize?"

"I was going to say 'match Henry at chess,' but I assume you can do both at once."

He laughed and caught her arm. "What's the matter? You were laughing and then looked so sad for a moment."

"Just thinking it will be hard to keep ahead of the children. I am not exactly an expert at geometry, and I did promise."

"Oh, I can teach them that."

"You can? I mean...I know you can, but are you

willing?"

"After eight years in the royal artillery? Best qualification I can think of."

"Was it dangerous?"

He feigned a blank look. "Geometry?"

She shook her head. "You know what I mean."

"Only if one of our own guns blew up. Generally the French guns had trouble finding our range. That's why we moved the guns so often."

"So you had a good chance of coming back. It wasn't like being in the cavalry or the infantry."

"I had a better chance than many. I don't see them, the men I knew during the war, except Frobisher, of course, who won't let me alone."

"I suspect he would be a little lost without you."

"Frobisher?"

"He has never really grown up. You were his commander and he still looks up to you, the way Henry wants to."

"A father figure? You make me feel old."

"A leader."

He took her hand. "Do you look up to me?"

"I do now that you are taking an interest in the children."

"But not because I'm a soldier."

"I could never accept it if you went off to war again. That would be far too costly for them as well as you."

"Do you imagine I would leave these children alone again with only servants for company?"

She pulled away from him. "I am a servant, though one who cares so much about them."

"I did not mean—"

"But we must remember that no matter how we

share their education, we can never share anything more. I shall see you at seven o'clock."

"And you will play and Charlotte will dance?"

"Yes, if you wish it."

\*\*\*\*

Miss Greenway had unbent enough to abandon her cap and wear a gown that would not have been out of place at a formal dinner. And he had nearly blurted out that he wanted their engagement to be real. How could he convince her he was serious about giving up the military life? He could sell his commission, for one thing, though it was worth nothing at the moment. It had hurt his leg to ride, but already he was feeling the muscles strengthen. Did he really want to give up his commission? He still got inquiries about returning to action. If he and Marian were to wed, the children would be safe with her. He could then do his duty without feeling that he was abandoning them.

Wyle mused as he went to his study and poured a small ration of port. He must take things slowly with Marian. He must not slip up and blurt out that he wanted her or voice any of the hundred endearments that bubbled up in his brain to say to her.

Of one thing he was sure. She was essential to the happiness of Charlotte and Henry. He could not risk driving her away, for their sake. Over time she would see that he could be a good father, even if he had to leave them again. But how much time did he have? The tide was turning, the French were retreating from Spain. He would give anything to be there at the final victory. Or would he?

That night she played country dance music and instructed Charlotte in the steps, to show how it went.

Marian hummed as she ran through the steps with Hill, then played for the couple while they imagined a dozen other couples were on the floor. Wyle laughed when Henry defected from the chess game and joined in, bowing to a fake partner. Watching their attempts was so much more fun than spending an evening with adults. Then Charlotte tramped on Hill's foot and he had to sit down for a moment. Marian paired Henry and Charlotte, but he was too short for her. Wyle got up and took a place across from Charlotte while Henry bowed to the phantom lady. As he suspected, dancing did not do much worse to his leg than riding. He felt almost as though he had a family for the first time in his life. After the dancers were out of breath Marian played some sonatas for them.

He tried to remember why his marriage had been so bad—Louisa's pouting, weeping, and self-pity. Was it because he was never there, or simply because she was a weak woman? But Marian wasn't like that. He could scarcely remember Louisa's face now except the hint of it in Charlotte's countenance, the mouth mostly. Thinking of Louisa no longer filled him with dread or guilt.

There had been no time for him to plead with Louisa. Her mind had been made up about her future, perhaps before she left England. And he had not gone to the dock to see her off. He was a soldier about to embark for the Peninsula and would be taking ship himself soon enough.

But before he left London, there came a letter from her cousin announcing Louisa's death. He felt devastated. In the very next post came a note from Louisa saying she was not dead but asking him to report that she was, and to send Charlotte to her cousin so she could have her daughter with her.

She also revealed that their marriage had never been legal since she was already married to the Comte before she and Wyle met. Initially Wyle had been shocked, then somehow relieved that Louisa was never his wife. But there was no way he would ship a child of his into the maw of war and so he wrote, to the cousin. With his head in a whirl and aching desperately, he had called the children from their lessons.

Telling the children about the fake death had not been the traumatic experience he had feared, and that had upset him. Charlotte had wept a little and Henry had asked to see her portrait. And no more was said of her. That's how little she had meant to the children. It was both good and bad. Good that they were not stricken but bad that they seemed to have so little feeling for their own mother.

He had a notion that if anything were to happen to Marian Greenway, even after these few days, their reactions would be quite different. He tried to imagine how he would feel if she left them, and the word was "devastated." So he must move slowly.

Chapter Seven

The next day they rode again, the children with less supervision than before. Marian knew a few qualms as they went ahead, with the groom leading the way to keep their horses in check. She wondered that Wyle stayed back beside her to make critical remarks about Charlotte's hands or Henry's seat when the information would have been so much more useful to the children.

"It is only their second ride, sir. Have some patience."

"Odd, I had always expected someone would be teaching them all this in my absence."

"And what was the case?"

"They had been made virtual prisoners by overcautious servants after my wife abandoned them."

"I'm so sorry. That must have been very painful."

"Less for me than for them when I finally accepted that she was not coming back. In fact, it was almost a relief."

He could not have shocked her more if he had said he'd murdered the woman.

"It can never be easy to lose one's mother."

"I thank God I prevented her from taking Charlotte with her. Had she spirited my daughter away, I might never have seen her again."

"Only Charlotte?" Marian wondered what sort of woman would favor one of her children over the other.

Wyle frowned. "She was ever Louisa's favorite. Her birth had not hurt as much as Henry's."

"So they have always been dear to you. It's just that you've been in Spain."

"A poor excuse for not making sure they were reared properly." He looked toward the center of the park, probably seeking to change the subject of his neglect. "How did you get word of your father's disappearance?"

"His commanding officer wrote to us. It was at the battle of San Sebastian. I take it not many cavalry were involved, but his troop was used for reconnoitering. His men reported he had ridden off toward the French position but never rejoined them. All returned safely by the end of the battle except him. They had thought him shot by snipers, but neither he nor his horse was found, so they assume capture."

"The war will be over soon. If he is being held by the French he will be freed."

She felt a desperate flutter of her heart. "If? But what other possibility is there?"

"You're right. Where else could he be?"

"I— Since you are so well informed, I'm sure you heard the rumors that he deserted."

"But I knew him. He would never do such a thing."

Marian felt herself smiling. "Thank you. It is a comfort to hear one who should know what he is talking about exonerate him."

"He must still be alive and able to speak for himself. The French don't tell us all the prisoners they hold."

"Again I thank you."

"For what?" He glanced at her.

"Hope. You must be the only other person on earth who thinks he might still be alive."

"Including your mother?" Wyle seemed rattled and glanced at the children, who were now besieging the groom with questions.

Marian bit her lip. "She always expected him to die in battle and gave him up for dead many times. I think she dares not hope."

"If only my opinion meant something. I suppose your mother gets no pension."

"No, nor his pay either. It's much like being in limbo for her. Hence my foray into service."

"But what about your father's estate?"

"Though the war office does not admit his death, my father's solicitor, under the lash of my cousin, has begun to probate his will. My uncle was to be executor. Indeed he was charged with the care of the estate in our absence, for we went with Father to the Peninsula. But since Uncle died in the interim, that *duty* fell to my cousin Cole Greenway, by what right I cannot fathom."

"Let me guess. He greased the palm of said solicitor and left you both destitute."

She shook her head. "Not exactly. He offered my mother a roof over her head provided I marry him."

"How generous."

She saw that dent of concentration between his brows, together with the severe line of his mouth. But it had nothing to do with the children breaking into a trot, so she and Wyle urged their horses forward as well. "He said the same thing but without the irony. I must have inherited too much of my father's pride, since I had rather earn my bread. I did well at my first position."

"I can imagine you did. Why did you leave?"

She found herself blushing. She did not want to tell him how Cole had come to the house and annoyed her employers about her until they virtually had no choice but to let her go. "Children have a way of outgrowing the need for a governess. Charlotte won't need me in another year or so. By then you will want to send Henry to school or get him a male tutor."

"Why should I? They already have Mr. Hill for religious instruction, not to mention Latin and Greek. Besides, they have fallen in love with you. They will always need you."

"You may change your mind about marriage and decide your new wife can handle their education."

"I think I already have."

She sucked in a gasp and inadvertently jerked a rein and jabbed her horse in the mouth, which was not like her. She patted the creature's neck. But the groom had returned to a measured walk and so did they all. "So you will not forever dodge your relatives' efforts to supply you with a wife?"

"I see now, after the way the children have taken to you, that I wasn't just depriving myself of companionship."

"Then you will want to cancel our fake engagement so you can look about you for a likely prospect. You don't want to appear fickle."

"No! Say nothing about this."

"But why not?"

"Because that is the only thing keeping me safe from every harpy in town."

"Harpy? I am not sure you are quite ready for marriage."

"I need much work, don't I?" He smiled sheepishly. "Perhaps you can give me a few pointers while you work with the children."

"Pointers? On what?"

"How to be more amenable to women."

She choked on a gurgle of laughter. "I shall try. But manners are best mended when a man is young."

Now the children both brought their horses smoothly into the trot in imitation of Reed.

Henry waved. "Father, look! I am posting."

"Excellent, Henry!" It was hard for Wyle to trot Warlock and match his long stride to that of her horse. After gazing at the children ahead of them, he turned back to her. "Alas, can a graybeard learn nothing?"

"You have already made much progress, changed so much. I do not despair of turning you into a marriageable gentleman if you will be advised by me."

"I shall be putty."

\*\*\*\*

After Marian finished the morning lessons, she assigned the children their translation and descended the stairs. Wyle's strange behavior in the park came back to her. He now wanted to look for a wife but only from the safety of their fake engagement. She supposed that made some sort of perverted sense. She was still dealing with it in her mind, trying to reason it out as a man would, when she entered the drawing room—to confront his Aunt Alva earnestly staring at Wyle.

"I'm so sorry. I shall return later." She retreated to the door.

"Marian, wait," Wyle said desperately.

"Miss Greenway," Aunt Alva said with delight. "I did not hear you arrive."

"I-I…"

"She was helping the children with their lessons."

"Oh, still having trouble getting a governess? Stay,

my dear, since this concerns you. I am throwing a ball to celebrate your engagement."

Marian turned an accusing glare on Wyle and seated herself across from him. He shrugged as though none of this was his fault.

"Is there anyone you would particularly like to invite?"

"No one."

Alva looked at her as though it was impossible to have no connections.

Marian licked her lips and shaped them into a severe line. "In fact I think it is premature to be thinking of balls."

"Don't tell me. Wyle has done something to give you a disgust of him." Alva wrinkled her brow as she waited for an explanation.

"More like something to make me doubt his reason." She wondered what she would say if pressed for details. The fake engagement came to mind, but it was one of the many things she could not speak of.

Alva shrugged. "Well, these little things will happen. It will work out." She consulted her lists. "Your mother is the wife of Major John Greenway. But Wyle tells me your father is a French prisoner of war."

"Yes, and my mother is not well. She never leaves Northampton."

"But we must send her an invitation anyway. She will be so happy for you. What is her direction?"

Marian glanced uncomfortably at Wyle. "Uh, Briarcliff Cottage, Tynbrill Down."

Alva made a note. "Very good. I perceive you have been taking care of her yourself and have only come for a brief visit. I can suggest a modiste for you. Where are you staying?"

Marian hesitated, glad now that she had forsaken her prim cap, though she still wore a dowdy gown of dark blue. She glanced at Wyle, whose eyes shifted desperately. "I am not satisfied with my current lodgings and mean to remove to another today, if possible." Was that a look of panic in his eyes?

"Well, you could always stay with me, you know. Here, I shall set down my address for you. Wyle never remembers it."

"Thank you, but—"

"I thought no more than three hundred."

"Three hundred what?" Marian asked, feeling the situation slipping beyond her control.

"Guests, of course."

She could feel her jaw drop, but when she glanced at Wyle he shrugged.

"Now, now." Alva patted her hand. "You handled yourself well enough in front of the family. This will be no very great matter. I shall send the invitations. What say you to two weeks from Saturday? No, you need to have a dress made. Say three weeks. It is early in the season, and there are plenty of good days left."

"Perhaps we should wait." Her voice came out as a strangled gasp.

"Nonsense. I want to celebrate your happiness. Wyle, I assume you have time to get the ballroom cleaned."

"You want to have it here?" Marian could feel the world whirling out of control.

Alva stood up and tramped to the door. "Of course. Where would I put three hundred people in my house?"

With that she whisked out of the room and Wyle

burst into laughter.

"You may think this is a great joke, but what will you do in three weeks' time when there is no Miss Greenway to present?"

"But she recognized you. So you can stop pretending to be just a governess."

"What? What are you talking about? I *am* a governess and a damned good one."

Henry entered at that moment with his translation, so she bit her lip on the hope that he had not heard her swear.

After lunch Wyle recommended they throw open the doors between the drawing room and the ballroom. He thought Charlotte's playing might help Henry learn to focus on his fencing.

Charlotte laughed. "Learn to focus under trying circumstances, you mean."

At any rate, the doors were opened so the girl could hear the clash of the fencing foils and Wyle could hear every wrong note Charlotte hit. Or perhaps not. Marian recalled how defective his hearing was, unless that was a ruse.

Her roles were blurring together, Marian thought, as she demonstrated keying to Charlotte. She'd walked into the drawing room as though she belonged there. Why hadn't he warned her? It was highly improper of her to be residing in this house as anything but a governess. If it came to be known she had stayed here without female chaperonage and then aspired to marry Wyle, the world would put the worst possibly interpretation on her actions.

**\*\*\*\***

Before dinner she always sent the children off to do

an hour or so of written homework. This was the perfect opportunity to have it out with Wyle. Even if he discharged her, he must be made to understand that this charade had to end. She knocked at the study door, but only Hill answered and disavowed any knowledge of Wyle's whereabouts. He needed him as well, to decipher some notes Wyle had made in his absence. She threw open the door to the library next door, but he was not there, just a ledger, with a pen drying on the blotter. She cleaned the pen. He could not be trusted even with small things.

She went into the hall and asked Trumby where Lord Wyle was. He indicated the stable as the likeliest place to look. Marian went down the back steps and was crossing the stable yard to that building when she saw his head above a tall yew hedge. He was pacing the small rose garden outside the breakfast parlor.

She let herself in by the gate and stood there waiting for him to see her, but he kept pacing, head down and with that mark of concentration between his brows. It was no more than twenty paces from the sundial in the middle to the corner he had chosen. The quadrants each contained a bench surrounded by roses, one shaded by an arbor.

She realized what he was doing, exercising his injured leg. Now that he was riding, fencing, and dancing, perhaps he'd been pushed too fast in his recovery. His head jerked up as he saw her.

"I was just admiring the garden," he said. "Never spent much time out here, but we have roses in abundance—or we will in three weeks. Not enough for the ballroom but certainly enough for the front hall."

"Are you insane?"

He grinned. "Well, yes, but generally regarded as harmless."

"Not in this case. You may think it a great lark to let this ball go forward, then not appear, but think of the repercussions for Charlotte. Think how your aunt will feel."

"I have every intention of appearing."

"Oh, no. Now I see your plan, you mean to use this as a public forum for ending our engagement."

He looked stricken. "How could you think I would do that to you?"

"Then what do you plan to do?"

He came and took her hands. "I have been trying to think how to say this to you without making you want to bolt. Three weeks does indeed seem like too little time. And you have only known me—what—four days? At the ball I would like to reaffirm the fact that I want to make Marian Greenway my wife." He drew nearer and gazed into her eyes in that compelling way he had, then stopped her complaint with a finger on her lips.

"But first there is something I must tell you."

"What is it?"

"I was never married to Louisa."

"You are insane."

"Listen to me. She was married to the Comte de Villars first. When she heard he had died in battle, she accepted the marriage her parents arranged to me."

"So you did marry her."

"In good faith, but she received word from her cousin that Villars had cheated death."

"That is why she went to Italy?"

"And stayed with him. Louisa asked me to tell the children she was dead."

Marian felt paralyzed. "Is this a joke?"

"It is the truth, finally. You may consign me to the devil if you like."

"She chose her husband over her children?"

"I…had not thought of it like that, but yes. She did—does—love Villars."

"But never to see Charlotte and Henry again?"

"She has sent a letter requesting Charlotte come for a visit."

"In the middle of a war?"

"Yes. It is out of the question at any time. I would never get her back."

"So you have this put on you along with everything else. No wonder you are not quite sane."

"And it is all coming to a head."

"How do you know she really married Villars?"

"Why would she lie about that?"

"You are so naive. Why would she tell the truth?"

"I have to believe it. Anything else would be unbearable. Think about it. The children love you. I love you. What could be more perfect?"

She backed away from him, but he did not let go of her hands. "If…if this had happened years ago when I had my come-out, it would have been perfect. If my father were not missing under a cloud of suspicion, it might have been perfect. If you were not a soldier, it might still be perfect. But we are where we are. I am a governess and you are a peer who may or may not be married to a living woman and who may die if you return to war."

He tightened his grip on her hands. "There is no gulf between us but what your fear puts there."

He sounded so Shakespearean he almost convinced

her.

"There is more than one gulf between us. Beyond even this stupid pretense in which we are engaged, there is the fact that I will never marry a soldier, not after watching what my mother has gone through, and indeed what Louisa went though."

"I am not a soldier at the moment."

"You still retain your commission."

"That is easy enough to fix if it bothers you that much."

She didn't know what to say, for she did already in her heart have a regard for Wyle, not to mention a ready sympathy. "I must think."

"Yes, take your time. Take two weeks."

"What a ridiculous statement." She felt herself torn between desperate tears and hysterical laughter and resented it. "This is impossible."

"No. This is perfect." He grasped her hands tighter.

"Hearing *you* say that confirms it is a crack-brained idea." Somehow a hasty laugh slipped out and he pulled her to him to wrap his arms around her.

"Sometimes those are the best ideas because they come from the heart and not the head."

"Thinking with my heart never brought me anything but unhappiness. And I am tired of it."

"Then wed me, be happy, be a mother to my children." He looked at her intently and slowly met her trembling lips with a warm kiss. Marian felt her resolve crumbling. She also heard the window to the breakfast parlor open and shot back against the rose arbor as though she had been burnt.

Henry peered out. "Dinner is ready. Trumby gave up looking for you."

"Excellent." Wyle took Marian's arm and conducted her inside as though everything was settled.

If the previous night's dinner had been her time to speculate on an attachment between Hill and Charlotte, then surely Hill was returning the favor tonight as his gaze flicked between her and Wyle. What must Hill think of her? That she was a fortune hunter would be the kindest appellation he could use. Once again they practiced dancing that evening. It was all such a whirl. It seemed to Marian as though she had been given a family for only a few days, that she had to enjoy them all quickly before they were snatched away from her. But why such portents of doom? Perhaps Wyle was right and their marriage could be perfect...

Before she went to sleep that night, Marian penned a long letter to her mother asking for advice. On the one hand, this was exactly the sort of situation her mother had warned her against falling into. What would Wyle's friends think if they realized she was a governess? What if he tired of her? She knew Wyle was volatile. Would it not be worse for the children to have a mother and father at odds rather than a calm and collected governess? Perhaps they could delay their happiness until the children were older. But that was not fair to Wyle. He might want more children. In fact, she wanted children herself, and she had to admit she wanted to have them with Wyle.

She put all her arguments for and against the marriage into the letter but could not write the one thing that should be most important. She did care for Wyle. She thought she was falling in love with him. Seen in the light of society, her marriage to Wyle would be to his disadvantage. Thinking of the four of them sitting around a table together or riding in the park, it did seem perfect. Thinking of having a babe of her own felt like a dream, a fairy-tale ending. That was the problem. What he offered seemed too perfect to be real. Life simply was not like that. At least her life wasn't. Until now.

Was it possible her expectations were unaccountably low because of all her misfortunes? Could she be happy with Wyle in this ready-made life? And if she refused him would she regret her decision forever?

Chapter Eight

Against all odds, it was another beautiful morning, and the children rode out ahead of them with the confidence of beings who had been riding all their lives. Wyle rode on her left side as though he had always been there and always would be.

"Have you thought about our discussion?" he asked without looking at her.

"I have thought of little else, sir."

She stared at his handsome profile. The sun showed the firm line of his lips but did not reach his eyes under his hat brim.

"And your decision?" he asked.

"Unlike you, I feel unable to bolt into a decision. I need to consider my mother."

"She could always live with us."

"Someone must take care of Father's estate when we get control back."

"You'll hire a bailiff." He was smiling now, but it was forced.

"You seem to have an answer for everything."

"There generally is an answer to every problem."

She looked up at the children between the ears of the horse. "But sometimes the answer isn't what you want to hear."

He looked at her now that she had his attention. "Don't say no."

"For now, I must."

"Please take time to consider."

"We must do something soon. Our rides will begin to cause remark."

"By whom?"

"By anyone who observes us, I imagine. Him, for example." She nodded toward one rider in particular. He was at a distance but he *was* watching them. She entertained the fear that it might be her cousin, but the clothes didn't look right, and she did not recognize the showy bay.

"He is just surprised to see Henry here. Most children do not have leave to ride in Hyde Park. You're just imagining people talking about us."

"You must admit we have not been discreet."

"We have done nothing wrong."

"Perhaps you have not. Rules are different for a woman."

"I hope you are not teaching Charlotte anything so nonsensical. Women now have just as many rights as men."

She pressed her lips together. "Because you are a fair man, you imagine what the world should be like, but it is not a just place. And when it is time for her come-out you may discover to your horror that people may shun her because of your second marriage to the governess who snared you."

"Then to hell with the lot of them. She's an innocent. If they won't accept her, I have no use for them."

"You have pressed me for an answer and I have said no. Before arrangements go any further, I should make my excuses in a letter to your aunt. Perhaps that my mother has taken a turn for the worse and I must go to her. Then, if the engagement dissolves, no blame will fall to you."

"You mean to leave?"

"Like you, I feel I must do something. I am just trying to avoid making a huge mistake."

"But remember what your father said. Have the courage to act even if you make a mistake. At least it will be your own mistake."

He rode away to catch up with Charlotte and Henry and to laugh at his son's ideas for what horse he should buy. Even though she had disappointed him, he could still feign happiness for the children. Marian felt distanced from them already. At least she had knitted this family back together, but she was not part of it, nor should she be, not with Cole on the loose to discomfit them. She did not want any of them, least of all Wyle, exposed to his rude manners and insistent intrusions.

\*\*\*\*

After the morning ride, Wyle returned to find Hill hard at work at the desk in the library.

"I fear I must burden you with even more busywork to distract you from what you think to be a great literary endeavor."

"And what is that, sir?" Hill looked up with a smile.

"Preparing the ballroom for three hundred guests in three weeks' time."

Hill froze and stared at him, the ink drying on his pen. "You're serious."

"Never more so. My Aunt Alva has decided to throw a ball…here."

"I see. So we need food and drink for three hundred, plus all the flowers I can buy in London. I shall make a note."

"If I said I was entertaining the Prince Regent you still would not bat an eye, would you?"

"I am yours to command. It's not my place to question."

"Nor mine when it comes to Aunt Alva. She's like a rock."

"And the occasion?"

"To publicly announce my betrothal to Miss Greenway."

That stopped Hill with his mouth open and his pen arrested above his notebook.

"You don't approve."

"Approve? It's not my place to approve or— I have to admit I had hoped some such relationship would blossom. She is so perfect with the children. But I had assumed it would take some time to explore each other's… I am truly treading on forbidden ground here. Just allow me to wish you happy, sir. There will have to be an announcement in the *Morning Post* and the…"

"No, not yet."

"Not yet? But if the engagement ball is in three weeks, we cannot wait. The invitations must go out soon."

"My aunt is taking care of that, so it will be a week before she gets them sent. I need a few more days."

Hill stared at him.

"To convince Miss Greenway," Wyle added.

Hill cleared his throat and placed his pen back in the stand. "Generally speaking, a proposal of marriage precedes the engagement party. You have asked the lady in question?"

"Yes, of course. We are in accord on almost every point."

"Almost? You make it sound like peace negotiations."

"She does not want to marry a soldier."

"Understandable, given the fate of her father. So you mean to resign your commission?"

"Yes, soon. It's unlikely they will need me again anyway. But I hate to be thought so weak as to let a few wounds deter me."

"There is one thing that worries me," Hill mentioned.

"What is that?"

"Miss Greenway's change in status from governess, which makes her unapproachable, to your fiancée. If you had a female relative staying in the house everything would be more proper."

"I should think a man of the cloth would be chaperon enough."

Hill shook his head with the disapproving line to his mouth that had prevented Wyle from one or two social disasters in the past. For one so young, Hill had a massive sense of propriety.

"You could, of course, ask your aunt to stay, the one who is planning the ball."

"No. I should never be rid of her."

"What about a female relative on Miss Greenway's side? That would be even better."

"I suppose I could ask her mother to stay. Better than inviting Aunt Alva, who once entrenched might never leave."

"Do you know Major Greenway's wife?"

"Not even slightly, but I have memorized her direction. Take a letter, Hill."

\*\*\*\*

After she had changed from her riding dress, Marian left her letter on the hall table to be posted. In the middle of French lessons, she decided not to send it, not to burden her mother. But when she went for it, the table was empty and the die was cast.

Instead of another art lesson, she decided to take Charlotte and Henry to see some art at the Royal Academy or possibly at the Society of Painters in Oil and Water-Colours, if she could determine their new location. Wyle had left the house on business, but when she consulted Mr. Hill, she was relieved that he seemed more than glad to escort them. But he insisted on a closed carriage in case it might rain.

When they were finally underway, she said, "I hate to take you away from your work."

"I have nearly caught up with Lord Wyle and all that he wrote while I was away."

Marian smiled. "Wyle has said I may read his memoirs when the work is closer to completion."

"We should both be glad for another eye in regard to punctuation and grammar, but would the battle accounts...forgive me. I am speaking foolishly to the daughter of a soldier."

"I want to read it too," Henry said.

"Yes, I want to read it as well," Charlotte reminded him.

"But you are not used to such grim fare," Hill protested.

"As though French grammar isn't grim enough." Henry's young face looked mutinous. "We have a right to read it."

"Don't you see?" Charlotte asked. "We are the children of a soldier just as Miss Greenway is. We need to share that with father."

Hill nodded but looked at Charlotte in a different way, as though he realized she was an adult now. Marian found herself smiling at how effectively her pupils had used logic to make an impression on Hill.

"I will speak to Lord Wyle."

As it turned out, Hill had a vast knowledge of art and was able to conduct Charlotte through the rooms with as much authority as Marian. She helped Henry analyze horse studies, though his motive was more to choose the best possible horse rather than the best possible way to paint it.

They spent so long over the watercolors and had such a good time they decided to leave the Royal Academy for another day and drove straight home. Wyle was not back, and Trumby inquired whether they should start luncheon without him. Marian hesitated, but when Frobisher presented himself clearly expecting to be fed, she decided they would have the meal on schedule. Hill nodded his approval, but her brave decision had been for naught since Wyle appeared before the first dish reached the table.

Where've you been?" Frobisher asked as Wyle seated himself at the table.

"Business. Some of us are duty bound."

"Disadvantage of being the only son," Frobisher said as he helped himself to the poached fish.

Marian had been busy trying to analyze why she had a dislike for Frobisher. It was not him sponging meals from Wyle or his running tame in the house. Such easy manners had endeared many subalterns and younger sons to her during her time in Spain. With a shock she realized it was his slight resemblance to her cousin, Cole

Greenway. If looking a bit like Cole could elicit such a negative response, it spoke much to the depth of her hatred for her cousin.

Seeing someone watching them riding in the park who resembled Cole had set her nerves on edge. She tried to calm herself with the reflection that Wyle could not be so easily put off as her former employers, but the threat or even the thought of Cole cast a pall over what should have been a happy day.

It was Charlotte who brought up the memoirs and made their case for being allowed to read them. Wyle looked at Marian and she nodded.

"Very well then. Once Hill has expunged my worst errors. But they are not finished yet. And I have no intent to publish them until the war is indeed over."

Frobisher looked bleakly up from his empty plate. "Am I in there?"

Wyle smiled. "Yes, but you show to advantage. I suppose you have a burning desire to read them as well?"

"No, not even remotely. I don't like to live in the past."

Wyle cocked an eyebrow. "But it's good not to forget the past. Otherwise how could we learn from our mistakes?"

Frobisher dropped the apple he had selected from the dish. "What mistakes?"

"I was speaking of my life, not yours."

Frobisher had been glancing at Charlotte in a way that turned Hill's mouth into a grim line. Marian was quite sure Wyle would never give her in marriage to a man old enough to be her father, but such things did happen. If his best friend asked permission to pay his attentions, would Wyle allow it? Suddenly she could see why having soldiers run tame in the house was a disadvantage.

If such a thing came to pass, Marian would intervene. That stopped her. As Charlotte's governess she had absolutely no right to speculate about the girl's marriage prospects. But as Charlotte's stepmother she would be in a position of influence with Wyle. She closed her eyes. She should not marry him just to protect his children. Or was that a good enough reason?

Hill's apprehension about Charlotte did not go unnoticed by Wyle. If she and Henry had not been invited to dine with the adults, Frobisher would still be thinking of her as a little girl. He hoped his lieutenant would not speak to him about making addresses to her. She was far too young for him and...he did not want her to marry a professional soldier.

The thought hit him like a cold drenching as they finished the meal. He did not want Charlotte to suffer the uncertainty Marian and her mother had gone through. Perhaps his profession had been part of Louisa's problem. Now that he looked at the situation from another point of view, he understood Marian's reluctance. All he had to do was resign his commission. Why was that so hard?

****

Alva appeared in the schoolroom midway through the afternoon, and Marian panicked. Fortunately they were finished with formal lessons, and Marian had worn a smart dress and no cap. But the children knew nothing of her dual role.

"Ah, Miss Greenway. Well met. Still helping the children, I see. Ready to go shopping?"

She felt speechless but hated to tell Alva she had

completely forgotten about the expedition. And what about the children? Did she tell them the same lie they had been living? They thought of her still as their governess. How would they feel about her as a prospective mother? Whatever she was going to do would have to be decided in the next few minutes.

"Just let me get my reticule. The children both have drawings to do."

"Perhaps Charlotte would like to go with us," Alva suggested.

There seemed little point in shopping at all, let alone taking Charlotte, but she could never say that. For once Wyle was going to have to get out of a tangle on his own. "Yes. It would be a good experience for her."

"And I don't see enough of the girl."

"May I go too?" Henry begged. "I'll be quiet."

"I think it would be a good experience for Henry as well," Charlotte said. "He needs practice being patient and waiting on women. Besides, even though he is not fond of painting, Miss Greenway says he has an eye for color."

"If you think so." Aunt Alva looked dubious about this, but Henry volunteered to carry word to the butler as to their purpose.

Somehow Marian would have to get Charlotte alone and explain about the subterfuge, not the whole thing but enough to get through the day.

Alva pulled out her guest lists and went over them while they waited for the carriage to be harnessed. Marian felt her heart flutter when Charlotte looked over her aunt's shoulder.

"What is the list for?" Charlotte asked.

"Did Wyle neglect to tell you? You father's

engagement to Miss Greenway."

Marian looked at the girl and discovered delight on her face instead of shock. Charlotte came and hugged her. "I am so happy. This has been my dearest wish. I will go get ready."

Now she was in the suds. If she jilted Wyle she would hurt Charlotte and Henry. Jilted Wyle? But they were not even really engaged. She felt the real world and the fairy tale he had knitted together coming undone in her mind. What if they went ahead with the ball so as not to disappoint Alva, then Marian just disappeared later with the excuse of having to take care of her ailing mother. Would that be so bad? It would only delay the inevitable, but it did not seem as deceitful as letting preparations go forward and then trying to cancel the party.

She knew what she was doing, trying to hang onto the fairy-tale part of it. Why had Cinderella run away from the ball? Because she did not want to be seen in her rags. But Wyle would never condemn her for poverty. Still, that figure she had seen on the horse at Hyde Park had the look of Cole about him. And if he had found her, life would not be a fairy tale but hell.

When Henry reported the carriage was in front of the house, he stayed to entertain his great aunt while Marian went for her pelisse and reticule.

"This is so exciting," Charlotte said on the way downstairs.

"I mean to ask your aunt if you may appear at this ball. Not dance, you understand, since you are not yet out, but be in the receiving line and perhaps sit with her through part of the evening."

"Oh, that would be wonderful."

"She won't agree right away, of course, but it does no harm to plant the seed."

"But she might agree. I shall act so mature today she will feel compelled to agree."

Marian laughed. "No, just be your sweet self."

They visited two dressmakers, ordering Marian's dress, a russet silk, at one and some muslin gowns for Charlotte at the second. The girl was determined to order a new riding habit so was measured for that as well and chose a deep green wool. Marian had paid for all her items in cash since she said she had not transferred her accounts to London yet. They put all of Charlotte's wardrobe on a tab the modiste seemed eager to start for them after the lengthy absence of Louisa from their shop. Henry spent all his time gazing out the window at horses.

"That lawn would make a nice ball gown for Charlotte someday," Alva said.

"I think we should have it done up for her so she has one, in case."

"In case of what?"

"In case her father agrees to let her attend your ball." Marian cast her gaze down toward her reticule. "There is small chance."

Charlotte must have realized what Marian was doing and took up her lead. "Yes, even though I am almost seventeen, Father can be so stuffy about things like that."

"Wyle? Stuffy?" Alva pursed her lips. "He has changed. I had lost track of your birthdays. Almost seventeen are you? But not for nine months, I make it. Still it would be a good experience, and in an atmosphere where no one would impose on you. Let me speak to him."

It was late when they returned, so Alva invited

herself to dinner and invited Miss Greenway as well. Marian was under the worst dread that one of the children would mention she dined there every night. Wyle was surprised and unnerved to encounter his aunt in the drawing room. She seemed a little shocked that they all were to dine together like country bumpkins.

"If they are to learn good table manners, it helps to see them in practice," Wyle quoted Marian.

Alva glanced at Wyle lounging back in his chair at the head of the table. "Assuming that is what they will witness. Charlotte, yes, could be allowed to dine with you, but Henry is far too young."

As though to give proof of this, the anxious Henry overturned his water glass, then let out an oath that he must have heard in the stable. At least that is where Marian hoped he had heard it.

She sent Wyle a panicked look in the midst of Alva's shocked gasp. He quite deliberately overturned his wine glass and swore vehemently as he blotted it with his napkin.

"Well!" Alva said. "I can see where the boy is learning his language, at any rate."

"Charlotte," Marian asked, "what is the protocol for spilled beverages at table?"

Charlotte rose. "Napkins will be laid flat over the spill," she said as she gently folded her napkin and placed it over the wet mark, "so as to cause the minimum disruption to the meal."

Marian was likewise covering the wine stain while glaring at Wyle, for he looked as though he was about to laugh out loud.

"Where did you read that?" Alva sputtered. "Minimum disruption? The meal has been ruined."

Charlotte turned to her aunt. "But if it were Lord Wellington who dumped his wine, you would cover the mistake for him and laugh. Once the white napkins cover everything, it's as though it never happened."

"Very good, Charlotte," Marian said. "Ah, here they come with the second course."

Trumby was breathing hard, probably worrying about water marks on the wood.

The older woman went silent since they were having salmon, which she particularly liked, and nothing more was said about Henry. The poor child sat rigidly as though afraid to move.

The rest of the meal passed off without incident, both children looking as though they were relieved to escape to the schoolroom, and Hill went similarly to the library. Alva had not finished yet. When Wyle followed her and Marian into the withdrawing room, she got Wyle to approve her plans for the ball's food, flowers, and musicians. Then she broached the matter of Charlotte attending.

Wyle looked surprised at her assumption he would not permit it, then Marian caught his eye and he tumbled to her scheme.

"After all the unfortunate scandal of her mother's abandonment, I hesitate to make even the smallest misstep."

Marian gazed heavenward.

"But I shall be with Charlotte all evening," Alva insisted. "There won't be the slightest chance anything will go wrong."

"Very well, if you think so. I trust your judgment implicitly."

"I must be off now. So much to do and so little time.

May I drop you somewhere, Miss Greenway?"

"No, Miss Greenway is going to review their written lessons, then stay for tea. The children will be down directly. Then I will send her home in my carriage."

"Very well. Remember your fitting is in two weeks."

When the energetic matron had been shown out, Marian realized that even now it was improper for her to be alone with him. She felt the need to make her position clear. "We were nearly in the suds today when Alva revealed the engagement to the children."

"But the children love you."

"And are not used to being consulted about such things so were not shocked."

"So all is well."

"Far from it. I cannot be both their governess and your fiancée."

"Have you thought any more about my offer?" He leaned his hands on the back of a chair.

She raised her gaze heavenward again. "I am seeking guidance."

He looked at the ceiling. "From whom?"

She was about to say "in prayer" but there was no need to lie to Wyle. "My mother."

"The way you say that, I think the cards may be stacked against me."

"I did not say I would take her advice."

"Then I do have a prayer. I will do anything."

"Will you sell out of the army?"

"Oh, that." He limped to the window.

"Why not sell out?"

"I'm not sure why I'm so reluctant. Perhaps I've been a soldier so long I don't know what else to do. I do not know what else I am. The shame of it is, I'm only good at killing."

"You are a father, and though you've had little enough practice, you seem to be quite good at it." Marian finally took pity on him and sat.

"Can't I be both?"

"That's like trying to be both dead and alive at the same time. When you go off to war, your life is forfeit."

He shook his head. "It's not as bad as that."

"It would be for me."

"But you would be safe here with the children."

"Yes, how convenient. So you could leave us with a clear conscience."

He turned to face her. "Are you telling me that if I don't sell out you'll leave?"

She thought for a long moment. "I very nearly left today when Alva revealed the presumed engagement to Charlotte."

Wyle staggered a little. "But you didn't."

"No, because Charlotte covered the disaster with her good wishes."

"So will you stay?"

"But only as their governess."

"You would be better able to protect them as my wife."

"Protect them from what?"

He glanced out the window at Alva finally getting into her carriage after a severe haranguing of Trumby. "Overzealous relatives."

"You don't think any of them would actually harm the children."

"Physically? No, but some of them might play at ducks and drakes with their fortunes. Not Aunt Flora, probably not Aunt Alva, though she is extravagant. But

Isabelle would like to get her hands in the pie. And there is no telling what Isabelle could talk Alva into. That's where I was today, trying to set up a trust they cannot break. It won't work unless you marry me."

"And you fear that as a governess I would not be able to fend them off."

"My aunts may like you, but Isabelle would find a hundred ways to make you miserable. And if Charlotte makes her come-out under the wing of Isabelle, since no one else has a daughter of marriageable age, you would not be needed. They'd send Henry to school."

Marian stared at him. "You're trying to frighten me into accepting you."

"I'm trying to make you see reason." He approached her chair.

"You're asking for a marriage of convenience."

"I'm thinking of my children."

"Is that enough to build a marriage on?"

"Many have survived that were built on shakier ground. Just say yes."

"I must do something. I cannot be both your fiancée and the governess. Too many people are watching me."

"Then become my wife."

He reached for her with his maimed hand, and she did not draw back. It was a strong hand for all that it had lost some of its power. He drew her to him and kissed her lightly on the lips, then the neck and the earlobe.

The rattle of the doorknob caused him to draw back. Hill came in with a sheaf of letters for him to sign. Marian occupied herself with the guest lists Alva had left.

"Oh, dear."

"What is the matter?" Wyle asked as he signed

documents he scarcely read.

"I just realized all these people that I know will wonder where I have been these last few years."

"Taking care of your mother, of course. Besides, you need not answer to any of them. Do you play tonight?"

"No, Charlotte plays tonight. I had thought that if she practices enough the next few weeks, she might play a piece at the ball."

"Hah, and you accuse me of living dangerously."

Hill laughed at them and lightened Marian's mood. Still, she did not know what to do. Her mother would counsel resigning, she thought. But for some strange reason she could hear her father saying, "Marry the man if he'll have you. Stop dithering about it."

Chapter Nine

The next morning, Frobisher's horse was standing saddled in the stable yard when the party came out the back entrance. Wyle strode to them saying, "You will have to ride with Hill and the groom. I must go to Woolwich."

"What has happened?"

"I just got word from Frobisher that they need my help at the military college."

Marian felt her heart jump. "They are recalling you."

"I can no longer pretend I am not fit for duty. I am merely to help train artillery officers and gun crews. Frobisher will be with me."

Marian did not ask the question, but it hung in the air between them like a large unanswerable gaff. Would he go to war again? She rather thought duty would drag him there rather than excitement enticing him, but no matter. He would be gone all the same.

And that answered the other question of whether she should marry him or not.

He looked up at her and said, "They need the new ordinance now. There isn't much time to get it ready. I shall have to do what I can. Will you take care of the children?"

She nodded but said nothing. There had never been any real choice for her, never a decision to make. Always the power was taken away from her—by the fortunes of war, by a cousin seeking to enslave her, and now by a man she held dear.

After Wyle and Frobisher rode off, Hill mounted Charlotte's hack now that her mare had arrived from Fair Oaks. The two paired off to trot abreast toward the park, and Marian came again to think the shy young man would be perfect for the girl. He might be a country parson, but he rode well and indulged her without patronizing her.

When they reached their favorite track, they ventured to go as fast as a jog and nothing untoward happened. After they returned to a sedate walk, Hill complimented Charlotte on her handling of the mare and Marian listened patiently to the catalog of all the horses Henry meant to buy when he was old enough. She knew in her heart she could not leave these two, but that did not tell her whether to marry or no.

When she ran the catalog of Wyle's flaws through her mind, the only one that stood out as important was his reluctance to give up military life. Beyond her fears for him lay something else that had been festering in her heart from the time she was a child. What was it? Yes, the sure knowledge that something was more important to her father than her mother and her. So Wyle also put duty before family.

Then she thought about what a difficult choice that must be for him, especially now that he was enjoying the children. Perhaps she was the one who was being selfish. Neither man needed to have fought in the war and had done it out of…what? Obligation, perhaps pride, and not a little out of the need for action. But to go back into it must take all the courage a man could muster, knowing what he might lose.

In the midst of her pondering on Wyle, Cole Greenway hailed her from one of the other tracks. His hack was the flashy beast she had seen the day before. Cole must have been in London for some days, since he was sporting a peacock-blue coat that looked ghastly stretched across shoulders so big. And his new hat did not entirely conceal the wild curling brown hair that stuck out above his ears. By the time he rode up, he looked disgruntled.

"What are you doing here?" she demanded in a fierce whisper. The groom Reed glanced back at them, then engaged Henry in discussion and led the boy ahead.

"When I heard what you were intending, I started searching for you. You cannot do this, hire yourself out as a paid servant again."

"You are the one who left me no choice."

"You never gave me time to discuss it with you."

"You made yourself perfectly clear." Marian tightened her grip on her reins. "Marry you or remain penniless." She could see Mr. Hill and Charlotte glancing back in some concern, so she smiled at them and vowed to lower her voice.

"Your father wanted me to take care of you."

"My father did not deed me or the estate to you."

"You are not capable of handling it."

"My mother and I would have had no trouble managing it if you had not usurped our power."

"If this is an example of your decision-making, I should have you declared incompetent."

"Is that your next step? That seems unfair, considering you forced me to seek employment."

Cole reached up to run one of his large hands

through his unruly hair—and almost knocked his hat off. "I never intended this to happen."

"And yet it has. How do you account for it?"

"You refused me before because you were in mourning."

"My father is a prisoner. He's not dead."

He shook his head sadly, playing, she realized, on her secret fear.

"You are wrong. You see, being in charge of shipping munitions, I have been able to make inquiries in France. There is no such person being held in any of the French prisons. Else I would have tried to ransom him or petitioned the army to arrange an exchange."

Cole sounded almost human when he said this, as though he really cared about her father, but then she remembered how good he was at acting the hero when he was no such thing. "I refused you because I did not love you. I still refuse you."

"If I had any idea how you felt…"

"I believe I expressed myself rather plainly. If you want to make amends, release the estate to my mother and my funds to me."

"If I do, will you forget about this governess position and come home?"

"Only when it is my home again."

"Very well." With that he rode off, never telling her what he meant to do.

Was there ever such an exasperating man? Of course Wyle tried her patience but in such a nice way there was no comparison.

They proceeded with the usual lessons that day, but all of them fell sadly flat without the exuberance of Wyle and with the pall of Cole's visit hanging over them. She had explained to the children who he was, but they also got from her sternness that she disliked her cousin.

The children felt her oppression and looked out the window for Wyle's return several times an hour. Marian was dreading the time for the fencing lesson, but Hill appeared, calling himself a poor substitute for Wyle. Henry was delighted to have a new opponent. Marian and Charlotte watched as they tested each other's skill.

They were all going upstairs to change for dinner, when Trumby informed Marian she had a caller in the drawing room. Having a grave suspicion that her mother might have made the trip, Marian opened the door to find Cole again.

"What do you want now? Did you follow me? This is unconscionable."

He came and took her hands. "I have done as you asked, or set the process in motion. Now will you reconsider?"

"I don't believe you. You plan to do the same thing you did at my previous situation. You will annoy my employer until he lets me go just to be rid of you."

"At least they saw reason."

"You lost me a perfectly good situation." She tried to pull away from him. "If you attempt such a farce again—"

The door was thrust open. "What is the meaning of this?" Wyle asked in his roughest voice. "Accosting Miss Greenway in my house."

"I am her cousin, Cole Greenway."

Wyle glanced at Cole's grip on her hands. "You are not acting like a cousin."

"That is because I have just asked Marian to become my wife."

"Impossible!" Wyle said, stepping up to them and forcing Cole to release her.

"Why is it so impossible?" Cole demanded as he looked Wyle up and down.

"Because she is engaged to be married to me."

Cole's jaw dropped and he spun toward her. "Is this true?"

Damn Wyle for pulling another rug from under her feet. "Let me explain."

"Well, are you a governess or this man's intended?"

"Both," Wyle said.

"And you accuse me of accosting Marian. Is this man's attentions welcome? Do you intend to marry him?"

Now she was trapped. If she said no, she was still on the ropes with Cole. If she assented, Wyle would take that as a definite yes. "It is you who left me little choice."

Cole looked from one to the other of them. "If this is true, there is no more to be said." He looked as though he were swallowing something large and sickening, his pride perhaps.

"There is more to be said," Wyle vowed. "Leave your direction with my butler. My man of business will call on you to arrange for the return of the estate that rightfully belongs to Miss Greenway and her mother."

"I see."

"What's that supposed to mean?" Wyle took a threatening step closer to the bigger man.

"You will take charge of the estate as her husband."

"No, her mother will be in charge, not that it's any of your business."

Cole turned on his heel and left the room without another word. Marian did not like the expression on his face. It was not defeated but angry, and she had no confidence Cole would comply with Wyle's demands.

"That's routed him. It's nearly time to change for dinner. Frobisher will be joining us."

"Why did you do that?" she asked as he turned with his hand on the doorknob.

"Because I don't like him and neither do you. Admit it."

"Very well. I don't like him, and having refused him once, I wasn't about to change my mind."

He took his hand off the knob and came back to her. "What are you saying? You didn't want my help?"

"He proposed before, and I managed to fend him off. After all, even with the family solicitor in his pocket he can hardly compel me to marry him."

"Most women would have fallen on the chance to be married when left without support."

She clasped her hands together for strength. "But I couldn't bear the idea of leaning on anyone."

"There's something else too, isn't there?" Wyle stood looking at her with concern.

Marian sat, suddenly feeling very tired. "He is the reason Mother and I returned from Spain. When my uncle died, Cole took over the estate. We received such disturbing letters from our estate manager that Papa thought we should come back."

"I see. You cousin pulled you away from your father when he needed you both with him."

"It was a shock to have Cole try to steal our estate, but I would not agree to marry him even after Papa was captured."

"How do you feel about Cole now?"

"He reminds me of that black time. Powerless."

Wyle sighed. "And I was very nearly as bad, with my aborted attempt at rescue. I made you feel powerless as well."

She stared up at him. "You trapped me."

He pursed his lips and stared at the floor, his jaw working. Then he knelt with such pain in his eyes she found she had to believe whatever he said. "It was not my intention. If you find you cannot like me either, then I will still fight to have your estate returned to your mother and you. Cole isn't the only one who can hire lawyers. Or would that also be unwelcome interference?"

"That I shall leave to my mother, who is more nearly concerned in the matter. She managed the estate during my father's whole career. When he was home, he didn't know what to do with himself."

"That is how I feel, as though I have outlived my usefulness. So I am writing my memoirs. Your father is in there, if you want to read that part."

"Really? Tell me something happy about him." Marian could feel the tears in her voice and desperately needed some good memory to hang on to.

"He was handsome, dashing, had to beat the Spanish women away with a whip."

Marian chuckled. "But faithful?"

"Eternally," he whispered, reaching for her hand.

"I am glad to hear it, for marriage to a military man has enough terrors without thinking about exotic women in foreign countries. I don't think I could ever bear what my mother endured."

"He was also daring in a careful way. He had courage but never led his men into traps. He was a good example to me."

"Then I have no fear to read your memoirs someday, all of them?"

"You spur me to finish."

Henry burst in then to recount how he had routed Hill, and Charlotte came along, joking with that young man. Apparently Frobisher had met them in the hall and was now sending speaking looks to Wyle about Hill and Charlotte. What an idiot Frobisher was on some things. If Wyle did not already realize the attachment, then he was dimmer than she thought him. And Wyle had apologized for trampling on her freedom. It was a start.

She stood, and Wyle managed it with a grunt. They would all be thinking he had proposed to her again. And all of them were smiling except Frobisher. Why did he not want Wyle to marry? It could mean a promotion for him. She shook her head as they went toward the stairs to change. Frobisher was the least of her worries.

Wyle watched Frobisher's attempts to engage Charlotte's attention during dinner that night meet with nothing but confusion from the girl. Hill, realizing what was happening, became almost monosyllabic. Charlotte blamed Frobisher, and rightly so. She ceased to draw the lieutenant out or even be polite to him, and the dinner ended with Frobisher drinking too much wine and recalling war stories entirely inappropriate for both Henry and Charlotte. Everyone except the two soldiers vacated the table after dinner. Wyle offered port in spite of his friend's condition.

"How much longer until Hill removes to the country?" Frobisher asked.

"His father will not retire until next spring. By then my memoirs will be done and I'll have less need of him."

"None too soon."

Wyle did not answer, still trying to fathom what he would do if Frobisher asked for Charlotte's hand.

"You understand why I say that?"

Wyle rested his chin on his fist. "No, I always thought you liked Hill."

"Your daughter is head over heels in love with him."

"Charlotte is still in the schoolroom."

"Exactly."

"What exactly?"

"He'll snap her up before anyone else gets a chance at her."

"You make her sound like a prize hunter."

"Surely you want her to marry within the *ton*."

"When the time comes, I want Charlotte to marry to please herself. I've had some experience in arranged marriages, and they don't always work."

"But he's just a country parson."

"What of it?"

"You can't be serious. With your fortune, Charlotte could look as high as she wants for a husband."

"I want her to be happy."

"Even if she marries Hill?"

"If she wants."

"If I had known you planned to throw the girl's future away, I'd have applied for her hand myself."

"Fro, we are classmates of an age. We serve together."

"Are you saying I am too old?"

"You are a career soldier. I have abandoned my children most of their lives because of the army. Charlotte does not deserve such a lonely existence for the rest of her days. Besides, we are in the same unit. We might both be killed at the same time."

"And yet you have proposed to Miss Greenway?"

Wyle rubbed his forehead. "Yes. I see your point. I should resign my commission if I want a settled life."

"The war won't last forever."

"Sometimes I think it will."

Frobisher stood up, rocking the chair. "I'm heading home."

"Not staying for tea?"

"I don't think I could stomach it."

Chapter Ten

Marian exited her room the next morning and encountered Wyle in uniform, the blue coat with red facings so easy to mistake at a distance for a Spanish uniform or even several of the French ones. To be sure, it was the blue colors of the Royal Artillery, but it was still a uniform. Had it been red, it would have broken her heart even more.

"Are you to go to Woolwich?"

"Not until later today. They are assembling the cannon, and I like to make sure that is done correctly. We will test fire them as well. I have to watch the youngsters to make sure they don't overload the cannon. I keep thinking they shouldn't need me, yet feel compelled to be there."

"Probably that geometry." She walked down the stairs beside him, determined to be brave and not berate him for his decision. Certainly she would not abandon his children, because he was doing his duty as he saw it. But she did not think she could compromise her beliefs enough to marry him. Then it hit her that she did love him and if he were to die, she would be as bereft as his governess as she would as his wife.

The children were just happy to have him with them again. Was it possible he could be both a soldier and a father? And a husband?

Once again Charlotte rode beside Hill, hitching her

too-small jacket closed with one hand as she managed the mare with the other. Henry struck up a conversation with Reed, the groom who regularly rode with them. That left her and Wyle to bring up the rear. In spite of disliking Wyle's compulsion to stay in the army, she could not deny a certain amount of pride in riding beside such a distinguished-looking soldier. If Wyle was torn about the decision, she could not blame him, for she was of two minds herself.

"Do you know if their mother is safe from the war?"

"Louisa was in France, last I heard anything of her, and she would have nothing to fear from British troops. Her count, I think, is still in service, though I heard he was again severely wounded at Vitoria. I had not thought much about them."

"Still, it must have been distressing to think of her in danger or actually dead."

"Or any other woman. But you have forbidden me to play the hero."

"I ask you to temper your exuberance with caution. I was impressed that you realized your error yesterday."

"And without you telling me. I'm a quick study. Give me the truth, Marian. Have I sunk beneath reproach in your estimation or is there a chance for us?"

She squeezed her eyes shut, but they were dry. She had left all her tears on her pillow. "I do not know."

"Well, it's a sure bet no one else knows," he said with a harsh laugh. "If you want control of the situation, you have it."

He sounded so desperate he almost did make her weep. "With control always come decisions, hard ones," she said.

"You didn't flinch from putting yourself in service.

It seems your next decision could be easier."

All she had to do was say yes or no. And yet she could not.

When they returned from their morning ride, Trumby informed Marian she had a caller.

"Oh, no. Do not tell Lord Wyle. I shall deal with this."

But when she entered the drawing room it was not Cole who awaited her but her mother. She looked strong and stern in the black garb she had adopted just in case she was in mourning and did not yet know it. Marian embraced her. After a few tears they pulled apart and looked at each other with smiles. Her mother's hair was still full and long, gathered under her hat, but streaked with too much gray for a woman her age. Her eyes had lines but were still sharp and alert. Whatever the war had done to her, it had not sapped her strength.

"Are you indeed happy to see me, Marian? You have so seldom asked my advice before. But for the first time in your life you sounded uncertain about what to do. I thought I had better come and assess the situation myself."

"But it is such a long journey."

"Not on the mail coach, which I could well afford since you have showered me with riches."

"Still, I am happy to see you."

"So explain this situation. You are the governess here?"

"Yes and the children are dears."

"But you are also engaged to Lord Wyle?"

"Not really."

"Marian, one is either engaged or not." Her mother removed her gloves a finger at a time and smacked them down on the table.

A gentle knock caused them to glance toward the door, and Marian said, "Come," expecting the generous housekeeper might have made them a pot of tea, but it was Wyle.

"Pardon me for the intrusion, but Trumby told me your mother had arrived and I think it would be fitting for me to welcome her as well."

"Mother, this is Lord Wyle. Wyle, this is Lady Elizabeth Greenway."

"If my daughter is indeed the governess here, then it would not be proper for me to appear as your guest."

Wyle bit his lip. "Shall we say Marian fills a double role in the household. How did you put it, Marian? That you have two faces, your governess face and your own, Miss Marian Greenway?"

"What exactly does that mean, sir? When I got your invitation, I was shocked."

"You wrote to Mother?" Marian shifted her gaze to Wyle, and he shrugged with his usual beleaguered look.

"Marian, help me out here," he pleaded.

"Oh, I wish I could, but I am at a loss as well. You invited my mother to stay here?"

"I had it from a very reliable source that it was the proper thing to do."

"Our Reverend Hill, no doubt."

"Perhaps I should start at the beginning," Wyle said. "Please do sit down."

"I can hardly wait to hear this." Her mother sat stiffly, and Wyle cleared his throat in discomfort as he began pacing the room.

"You are not the only one in suspense," Marian confessed, for she had no idea what he was going to say.

"In a nutshell, when Marian first arrived, I did not realize she was the governess but instead thought she was an actress hired by a friend of mine to impersonate my fiancée. So that first evening, I introduced her as such to friends and family."

"As an actress?" Her mother sounded more angry than shocked.

"No, as my intended."

Lady Elizabeth was speechless for a full minute, then shifted her gaze away from Wyle's sincere face to Marian's. "You allowed this?"

"I had no idea what was going to happen and thought I was dealing with a lunatic but a lunatic who paid well. So I determined to survive the evening, then put the relationship on the proper footing in the morning."

Her mother nodded but into the ensuing silence prodded, "And have you?"

"I am the governess to the children, but Wyle's relatives, Aunt Flora and Aunt Alva in particular, still think I am his fiancée."

"Staying here?"

"No they have no idea I am staying here. That would be very improper."

"But not if you are in residence," Wyle added with a nod. "Hence my letter." He opened his palms as if that solved everything.

"What? Am I to lend credence to this arrangement, which at best is a deception and at worst will rob my daughter of her character?"

"I had planned to cry off at the end of the season and disappear," Marian hastened to say.

"Disappear to where?" her mother demanded.

"My country estate," Wyle supplied.

Marian glared at Wyle and he had the grace to look abashed.

"Absolutely not. That would be worse than this. I realize, Marian, that having been country-raised, you enjoyed an independence not granted to most young women, plus the freedom of the war, but I will do everything in my power to put a stop to such an inappropriate arrangement."

"Even though I have changed my mind about the fake engagement?" Wyle asked.

"What?" Lady Greenway asked.

"Marian, I do care for you and want to marry you. The children adore you, and I see no impediment."

Lady Elizabeth stood. "Sir, I see a great many."

Wyle sighed. "Is it unheard of for a widower to fall in love with the governess and make her his wife?"

Her mother shook her head. "No, but that woman is writ down as a scheming fortune hunter."

"But Marian has her own fortune."

"In point of fact, she does not have it and is unlikely ever to lay hands on it."

"I have a competent solicitor and I intend to see what he can do toward putting Cole out of power."

"How very noble of you, but until then Marian must come home with me." She rose and started toward the door.

"Leave the children?" Marian wailed. She came to her feet and looked around desperately at what she had come to think of as her home.

"It's all been backward for us, Marian. Don't discount my suit until you have given me a chance to woo you. And the only way I can do that is if your mother agrees to stay."

"Woo?" her mother asked. "If I may remind you, sir, you are not just any widower but a man whose wife fled her home and abandoned her children to get away from you. There has been nothing to compare to the scandal in years."

"Lady Elizabeth, if I had met Marian in the ordinary way at a ball or some other public place, would you discount my suit?"

She sighed heavily and shook her head. "No, of course not, unless insanity does truly run in the family."

"It's only that his aunts are so insistent that he marry."

"I am not unsympathetic, but to have you change from a governess back into a society miss is not a transformation that will do you credit, nor will it be believed."

"But no one knows about the governess except the servants," Marian said.

"And no one knows Marian Greenway as my fiancée except my relatives. So if you agree to stay as her chaperone, she can live in this house as the plans for the wedding are finalized."

Lady Elizabeth looked at him dubiously as she clutched her reticule. "The wedding that is or is not going to take place?"

"Yes," Wyle said.

"No," Marian argued.

Wyle took Marian's hands. "I thought we agreed I have a chance to woo you."

"I have agreed to nothing." Marian clenched her hands into fists.

Her mother pressed her fingertips to her temples.

"At this point I understand nothing."

Marian gulped. "So, I do have to make a decision, and I have finally run out of time."

"We never had much time. If you are worried about Marian being alone with me, I assure you we have scarcely had a moment of privacy for conversation except when trotting about on the backs of horses. Any other time, a child, a servant, a relative, or an army of acquaintances is bursting in upon us. Which puts me in mind of my errand and the reason for interrupting you two." Wyle looked anxiously toward the door. "The thing is, my aunts have invited themselves to lunch today, along with cousin Isabelle, and I must produce Marian one way or the other, either as my fiancée or as the young woman with the good sense to jilt me and escape the lunacy of this household."

Marian stared at him and a strange bubble of laughter at the absurdity of the situation threatened to burst forth. "Why did I not know about this luncheon?" Marian demanded. "Even as your pretend fiancée it would have been a good thing to have told me."

"Because I forgot to open the mail until just now."

Suddenly Marian's mother did break into laughter. It was somewhat hysterical laughter, but it was laughter. "Very well, before this goes any further, Marian, is there a particle of truth in what he says?"

"Mother, do you think anyone could have made that up?"

"Let me rephrase. Is there the slightest chance you might want to marry Wyle someday? Because if you leave now and break the engagement, that all ends."

Marian gulped. "Under ordinary circumstances a proposal from Lord Wyle would have met with my approval. And now that I know him, I strongly feel he needs a responsible…"

"What? A governess?" her mother prompted.

"No, a keeper, but I suppose a wife will do."

"So you will marry me?" Wyle asked.

"Yes, I will marry you."

Wyle lunged toward her to plant a kiss but hesitated. "With your permission, Lady Greenway?"

"Very well, but be brief if you indeed have aunts about to assault your home."

He kissed her then, warmly and chastely. Marian realized that she had fallen in love with him even though she had steeled her heart against such a possibility.

There was a desperate knock on the door. "Sir, oh sir, they are coming up the outside steps now."

"Now, please come meet my family," Wyle said.

"In my traveling clothes?"

"You look splendid, madam, but on the off chance you would be staying, I instructed them to carry your baggage to the chamber that adjoins Marian's. We will await your pleasure."

Lady Elizabeth opted to change her wrinkled traveling dress for fresh garments without thinking that her hasty packing meant they were all equally crushed.

"No matter," Marian said as they stood over her mother's valise in the shared dressing room. "We are the same size. I'll get you one of my dresses."

"Just tell me, has he been a gentleman this whole time? I mean, the connecting door…"

"Wyle has never done a thing that would frighten me or compromise me, which is more than I can say for my cousin. And I do love Wyle."

Her mother came into her bedroom to clasp her by

the arms. "But dear, he is a soldier."

"I know. Who better than a soldier's daughter to cope with him?"

"This is the last sort of marriage I would have wanted for you."

"But admit it, you like him too."

"I admit that he needs you. He's so endearingly incompetent, except perhaps on the battlefield."

"And the war *is* almost over."

"That much closer to finding out if your father—"

"Yes, I know. But if Papa were dead, I would feel it, and I do not."

"I wish I had your faith. Come, let us not keep them waiting. Oh, I don't know about lavender."

"Papa is not dead. Wear the lavender and the silk shawl."

"All those buttons. We will be late."

"Oh, I think we should let Wyle stew in his own juices until you do your hair."

"I may be a firm woman, but I am fair. The hair is well enough."

When they entered the drawing room again, Aunt Flora rose and came to embrace Elizabeth, which surprised everyone else in the room except Lady Elizabeth.

"Forgive me the familiarity, but it has been so long. We were once so close, but family tends to tear you away from even your dearest friends."

Marian's mother returned the kiss on the cheek. "My fault as well for not writing, but I was ever a poor correspondent."

"So it is settled between these two?" Flora asked.

"Yes, and I think they will suit each other very well."

As they exchanged greetings, Alva started to babble about the ball arrangements and Isabelle got a sour look on her face.

"Such balls are usually given for young women just out of the schoolroom. I think it highly inappropriate to do so for a lady not in the first blush of youth."

Everyone turned to see how Marian would react, but she laughed. "So I have been telling them. A quiet wedding would be far more to my taste."

"But Wyle wants a ball, don't you, Wyle?" Alva pleaded.

Marian glanced at him to see if he was indeed a brave man.

"After my past experience with marriage I was hesitant, but as Alva has pointed out, it is an opportunity to get recognition for Charlotte. And I think Sophie too, though she is out, would attract many admirers among the three hundred invited."

"Charlotte is to attend?" Isabelle asked. "That's unheard of."

"Only as a treat to watch the dancing," Alva said, "and she won't go in to supper."

"I still think it's absurd."

Flora cleared her throat. "I think it's a *fait accompli*. Alva has already sent the invitations."

"Well, I didn't get one yet," Isabelle sniped.

Flora turned to Alva, who blushed and went on about the flowers. Marian knew for a fact that Alva had not got round to writing invitations yet. Was this Wyle's revenge on his aunt? If so, it might cost them, for she was sure that Mr. Hill, as well as she and her mother, would be pressed into service writing the cards.

Trumby opened the double doors and Wyle said, "If

that's all settled, it appears luncheon is ready."

An hour later, Marian left the dining room with her head spinning and felt ill equipped to teach the children anything that afternoon. Too much had happened too fast. She recalled something her father had said: "When everything is going your way, brace yourself for an upset. Chance does not favor anyone overmuch." Would it be Cousin Isabelle? Marian left her mother to rest while she went upstairs to the schoolroom for the art lesson. Charlotte's still life in watercolor and Henry's attempt to copy a horse drawing in pencil gave her leisure to ponder just what could go wrong. A note was brought, and she read it while the footman waited. In Cole's crabbed hand he invited her to meet with him to discuss her future.

"Is the servant still waiting?"

"Yes, miss."

She wrote that under no circumstances would she see him. Her mother was in residence now and he was to leave them in peace. "Give that to the man."

She was curious what Cole could possibly have to say to her but not enough to endure another conversation with him, especially in the lobby of the Barclay Hotel. Nothing could have been more improper unless it was the situation she'd just escaped by agreeing to marry Wyle. If Cole babbled about that to even one member of the *ton*, she was still in the suds.

Dinner was another lesson in table manners. That was the excuse Marian gave for having the children present at the table and for dining so early. It was a fiction she was sure her mother saw through but was too generous to say so. For Marian to be alone at table with Wyle and Mr. Hill, though a clergyman, would have been beneath reproach.

She glanced at her intended and won an endearing smile from him as he tried to show Henry the difference between the forks. Wyle was a good father when someone showed him what his children needed. He was actually a very patient teacher, so he would probably do well at Woolwich. She did not like that he would be away frequently, especially now with her changed circumstances. Even though she was his fiancée staying in his house with her mother for chaperone, she should not be receiving his callers, not even his aunts.

Twice during the meal her mother called her to task for being inattentive. At the end of it the children left them to work on their lessons. Each expressed again their delight at meeting her mother.

"I must say they are the best behaved young people I have ever encountered. You could not have waved a magic wand and done that in the space of a week, Marian."

"No, they were always well-behaved and dutiful. Perhaps their military upbringing?"

Wyle smiled. "I was not here enough to have swayed them one way or the other and can take no credit. But I have always engaged the best governess I could find."

Hill nodded. "Soon Charlotte will be launched into society and Henry will be off to school."

"Yes, my tenure here would have been short. A season or two."

"But now it will go on forever." Wyle smiled again. "Shall we toast to our changed circumstances?"

"Normally ladies retire to the drawing room at this time," her mother said.

"Then we will join you there, for I hate to drink

alone and Mr. Hill does not imbibe."

"I think I might make an exception in this case," Hill said. "We do have cause for celebration."

"Yes," Elizabeth said as they waited for Wyle to pour. "We have all managed to conceal Marian's transition from governess to your fiancée. I compliment you, sir, on the devotion of your servants."

They touched glasses even as the dent between Wyle's brows became more pronounced. "What had my servants to do with this hard won battle for Marian's hand?"

Marian shook her head. "I should have thought of that before. If even one of them, down to the youngest housemaid or under groom, had gossiped about me, it would be all over town by now. They must all be devoted to you and the children. And you *can* take credit for that."

"I had no idea we were in so much danger."

As Hill moved to escort Marian, Wyle downed his wine, slid out of his chair, and took Lady Elizabeth's arm to walk her across the hall to the drawing room. "I have convinced my relatives that our acquaintance is through Major Greenway and is distant but of long standing."

"But we met you only once in the Peninsula, and we said nothing of the kind," protested Lady Elizabeth.

He seated her in the best chair and took the sofa next to Marian. "No, of course not, but that is what they think. And what they think right now is far more important than the truth."

"Nothing can be more important than the truth," Hill said.

"In London society, nothing could be further from the truth," Wyle replied. "We have won over Aunt Flora and Aunt Alva, my most forceful aunt. Nothing else matters since she will roll over the rest of the family like a lumber cart."

Marian laughed at his apt description.

"I still don't like the pretense. Marian, you haven't said a word since dinner or even during dinner. Can you support this role?"

"I think I must now. There is no turning back."

"Would you wish to turn back?" Wyle asked.

"No. But I have the strangest fear that something may prevent all Aunt Alva's fantastic plans."

Hill smiled. "Now that your mother is in residence, what could possibly go wrong?"

Marian was thinking of Isabelle, of course. The temptation of showing Sophie off at a ball would be nothing to the possibility of routing Marian altogether and perhaps snatching Wyle for her daughter. If Isabelle ever found out about Marian's dual role, all would be over. And that could still happen, she reminded herself. They could trust Hill and if the servants had not snitched until now, they were safe. But what if Cole spouted off about it? She didn't think he went about in society much, but it took only one whispered comment.

Of course, Wyle would still marry her no matter what was said of her, but the scandal would cling to Charlotte. Suddenly it struck her that Wyle might never have intended to bring Charlotte out. Had he been so bitter about Louisa abandoning them that he would deny his daughter the chance to try her wings in society? Of course Charlotte's appearance would call Louisa to mind, but Charlotte should not be punished for that. The introduction of a virile and agreeable young man running tame in the house might be intentional. Mr. Hill was above reproach, and if Charlotte fell in love with him, Marian had to admit it might be for the better.

## Chapter Eleven

They had agreed to ride together after breakfast the next morning, but Charlotte invaded Marian's room in tears. "I have split the jacket of mother's riding habit, so I cannot go. Oh, when will they have my new green one finished?"

"Don't cry. You can wear my old one. It's worn but should fit you."

"Oh, Marian, you are the best of governesses and will make the best of mothers." Charlotte quickly changed her skirt and slipped on the buff riding coat. "I'd rather ride without a jacket than miss riding with Lewis." Then she blushed.

"You mean Mr. Hill."

"I must remember to call him that in public."

"You are young to be making such an attachment," she said but seeing Charlotte's discomfort she added, "but Mr. Hill is the very best man I could wish for you."

Charlotte laughed and then sighed. "Will I be allowed?"

"Have you any idea how your father feels about him?"

"He educated Lewis and helps in the care of his parents. He intends the living at Fair Oaks to be his someday, as well as the parsonage. Don't you see? I would never be far away if I married Lewis. It would be perfect."

She said this so much like Wyle that Marian had a qualm. "But staying close to your father is not your only reason? You do love Mr. Hill?"

"More than anything. I suppose I will have to go through the motions of a London season to please Father, but I'd as soon not."

"If you truly love Hill, waiting a year and enjoying yourself will not turn your head. Now get your hair pinned up or we will be late for breakfast."

The ladies were in time for tea and buttered toast, though Henry had finished the scones. Marian's mother and Mr. Hill were laughing at Henry's description of other treats Cook made when Trumby brought a message that Wyle immediately cracked open. Marian was getting used to seeing him in his uniform, a constant reminder that he also played a dual role. If she were a romantic miss she would see only the dashing war hero, but she knew the danger the uniform signified to all of them.

After reading the missive several times with that dent of concentration between his brows, Wyle looked up at them. "It appears I must get to Woolwich immediately. I just had a session with the new recruits yesterday and they all seemed promising, but this reports they have nearly blown up one of the new pieces."

"Is the note from Frobisher?" Marian asked.

"It must be, though the handwriting seems more legible than I recall his being. He also says I will be asked to command the new unit. I never discussed that with my superior, and it's unlike him to make such assumptions."

Marian sucked in a breath. *Did he not mean to resign after all?*

"Would you mind so much taking the children riding with a groom, Marian, you and Mr. Hill?"

"Perhaps we should cancel the ride for today?" she asked.

"Oh, must we?" Charlotte pleaded.

"Cancel? Of course not," Wyle said. "It's a beautiful day and there is no need for all of you to miss a ride."

Wyle limped to the door and stood with his hand on the knob. Marian could see the light of excitement in his eyes. Then he noticed her and returned a pleading look.

"May I speak to you for a moment?" he said simply.

She rose and followed him out to stand in the back hallway.

"If they truly need me…"

"Your children need you."

"The war is almost over. Charlotte and Henry can do without me for a few months."

"And what about the occupation? Even if victory is close, you are like to be posted to France for some time."

"I'll resign my commission as soon as we win. Besides, the children have you now."

"I'm small substitute for a blood relative."

"Before I leave I shall have you made their guardian, in case…"

"In case you are killed." She turned away. "That's why I vowed never to marry a soldier."

"You knew what I was. Marry me now. I can arrange it before I leave."

"Won't they all be shocked?"

"We are going to be married anyway. The children both accept you."

She whirled toward him. "Is this why you asked me to marry you, because I'm good with the children?"

He looked shocked by the accusation. "You don't just have two faces. You are two different people, the playful, joyful girl I have come to love and the cowardly one too afraid to live."

"You accuse me of cowardice because I do not want to stay in England waiting to hear of your death?"

"I know." He blew out a breath and gave a tired smile. "Whereas the real Marian Greenway would go with me if she could."

"My mother and I did go with Papa to the Peninsula. We were some use to him and the other soldiers. Now he is captured—or dead—just as Mother predicted."

"Had you been there, you would not have been able to prevent his fate."

"I could have searched for him. I would at least *know* his fate," she whispered desperately.

"Or perhaps not. We cannot know how things will turn out."

She felt her jaw clench. "But men seem to enjoy uncertainty like gambling. Only this is with your life, and your children's future."

"I need you to be courageous. I need you to be the Marian who will face any fear for me, even that one."

"Why should I? If I am prudent and scornful of love, it is because life has taught me how much love hurts."

He covered the space between them and wrapped his arms around her. "I asked you to marry me because I love you. I know that even if you accept me it may only be for the children's sake. For you do love them. It's in your eyes."

She looked up into his face, an accusation on her lips. "How could you think that I would marry you only for the children?"

"You accused me of worse."

"Yes, I suppose I did." She rested her head on his

shoulder and clutched his sleeves.

"Just as you have been put off by men, especially soldiers, I have not had the best experience with women."

"One would think that would make us ill-suited."

"Actually it makes us the best match and the best of parents. If you marry me before I leave, it will make it safer for them. No one else but your mother need know about the extra ceremony."

"You are going to be a soldier still, and I said I would never marry a soldier."

"And you have never broken your word even to yourself. But I promise you I will resign my commission."

"But you are a soldier before you are a father, certainly before you are a husband."

"Indeed, I was a soldier before I was anything else, but I am a man first. This is just my duty and will not last much longer."

"Possibly long enough to get you killed."

"If you fear that, all the more reason to marry me. It isn't just my children I want to take care of. I regard you and your mother as family now."

Marian found herself on the point of the worst decision in her life. "Perhaps one should not say never." She looked up at him.

"When one's father has disappeared into the maw of war? Who could blame you? I will say no more but wait for your answer."

"Very well. I am willing if it will protect them, but what about your family?"

"They need never know of it. All Alva's plans for an engagement ball will not be spoiled and we will be married again, when this is all over, in a ceremony the family can witness."

She grasped him by the shoulders and kissed him on each cheek. "You have my orders to survive somehow. I do not want to have to deal with them myself."

"Though you very well could. You have my promise that I will return."

He looked both ways in the hall, then tipped her head back for a real kiss. She hoped it would be one of many. Just as she was about to follow him out the back door, the front knocker was pounded and the butler opened the door to Cousin Isabelle.

Marian stifled the groan that sprang to her lips as the woman entered the front hall.

"Ah, I've caught you in," Isabelle said.

Wyle cleared his throat. "Isabelle, I really must go."

"It isn't you I want to see but Miss Greenway."

"I have promised the children a ride in the park."

"Oh, the grooms can take them, can't they, Wyle? And that nice Mr. Hill."

"Yes, of course, but Marian enjoys these rides as well."

"I see." Her affable smile crashed into a frosty glare.

"It's all right, Wyle. If you are content to trust them to Hill and the groom, I'll stay in. Will you take some tea?"

"That would be delightful."

When they went into the drawing room, Marian's mother was just finishing the *Morning Post* and rose.

"I shall leave you to your guest."

"Oh, please stay," Isabelle said. Her pale complexion was drawn tightly across her bones as though she'd been under a strain. Her face had more lines than Lady Elizabeth's.

Elizabeth moved to a sofa in the alcove and Marian followed them, completely forgetting to request the tea she had offered. To her surprise, it appeared within a few minutes. The servants had no more exited the room than Isabelle looked at Marian and said, "We all know this arrangement is not right."

"I beg your pardon?" her mother said.

"What is not right?" Marian asked as she poured for the others and added far too much sugar to the one intended for Isabelle.

"Your marriage to Wyle. After all, he is a peer of the realm. And your father is a common soldier."

"My husband is a major. He outranks Captain Wyle." Marian's mother sampled her tea with milk and smiled.

"And there is talk that he may have defected to the French."

"Ridiculous."

Marian went on pouring tea with a degree of calm she did not think possible. Would anyone blame her for upsetting a cup on the woman's lap?

"I do not know what hold you have over Wyle, but this simply will not do."

Marian handed her a cup. "How odd for you to think so. All his other relatives seem delighted that he is getting married."

"There are plenty of suitable young ladies for him to marry." Isabelle took a sip and gagged, then put the cup down.

"Sophie, for example?" Marian suggested.

"Wyle has known her all her life." She pressed her handkerchief to her lips.

"How odd that he did not choose her, then. Perhaps he regards her as too closely related or too young."

"I blame the army."

"For Wyle's preferences?" Marian took a sip of the hot brew, trying to calm her nerves.

"Perhaps he feels he owes your father something."

"I assure you, I did not trade on Wyle's acquaintance with my father."

"And to be staying here. I call into question Wyle's judgment. Men tend not to observe the niceties ladies must."

"Does my chaperonage mean nothing?" Elizabeth asked.

"You can't be awake all the hours of the day and night."

"What? I assure you nothing is going on, and it's insulting for you to suggest such a thing."

Marian had enough. To think she had given up a ride to listen to this nonsense. She cleared her throat. "Men do practice in their dealings a directness I find refreshing." Marian took a sip, seeing the worried face of her mother over the rim of her cup.

"What do you mean?" Isabelle asked.

"Marian, I don't think—"

"If we were men and you had offered me no fewer than three serious insults in the space of as many minutes, I would call you out, we would meet at dawn, and one of us would cease to exist."

Cousin Isabelle choked. Marian found herself hoping the cough would be fatal, but unfortunately the woman recovered her breath.

"How dare you!"

"Why would I not dare? Keep in mind my father did

teach me to shoot, in case I would meet someone like you."

"I know when I have been insulted." Isabelle stood up and shook out her skirt.

"Your understanding is more acute than I thought for someone who calls at this hour of the morning."

Isabelle's gown rustled ferociously and the door slammed behind her.

"My dear, that wicked temper of yours." Her mother shook her head. "You got rid of her, if that is want you wanted."

"She made you angry as well."

"Yes, you are right. If you had not put her in her place, to be sure, I would have. Find a groom and you may be able to join the party in progress."

"Perhaps I will, since I am still dressed for it." Marian rose and went into the hall, but the clatter of hooves in the courtyard alarmed her. Surely they would not be back so soon if something was not amiss.

When she flung the back door open, the four horses were riderless, and two under grooms were gathering up the reins.

She ran down the steps. "Hoby, help me mount. You mount and come with me. Jenkins, harness the team to the carriage in case someone is injured, then put those horses away."

The words were no more out of her mouth than she turned Charlotte's mare back down the alley and loped her through the streets. It wasn't a safe practice, but this was an emergency. One of the children could well be dead if they had lost control of all the horses. What did she care for her own safety or reputation if something had happened to one of them?

When she and Hoby got to the park, it seemed deserted in the early morning stillness, so she set the mare into a gallop along the track they usually took. One figure on the ground resolved itself into the groom, Reed, sitting. Then she saw the prone body of Mr. Hill—but not the children. Perhaps they had gone for help. As she galloped up, she could see Reed attempting unsuccessfully to stanch a leg wound. How on earth...?

She did a running dismount that she would not have thought possible, had she thought about it, and flung the reins to Hoby. The scarf around the brim of her hat could serve as a tourniquet. She knelt on the gory ground and bound the leg while looking anxiously at Mr. Hill.

"Have the children gone for help?"

"Abducted, by Gawd. Who would have thought it, poor mites."

"What? Who took them? Who?"

The pale man licked his lips. He was the next thing to unconscious. "It was a hired carriage, and I heard French spoken. Shot me off my horse and clubbed poor Hill when he tried to protect them. Bordeaux..."

"The bleeding has stopped, miss," Hoby told her.

"Half a dozen French coves. Gagged and bound them. Then stuffed them in a carriage."

"But why?" She reached for Hill and felt his heart. It still beat, but he lay as still as stone.

"Ransom, I suppose."

"This is insane. I must think."

Wyle's carriage pulled up then. All the footmen they employed began loading the injured groom and Hill.

"Hoby, listen carefully. Everything depends on you. Ride back to the house and tell Trumby to send for the surgeon and also the local magistrate. Then you must find Lord Wyle and apprise him of the situation. Do you know how to find him?"

"Aye, miss. I've been to Woolwich. Leave it to me."

"Tell him what Reed said about them speaking French. He may wish to ride to the port and get the harbormaster to check all shipping about to depart."

Hoby raced off, and Marian supervised the position of Reed in the coach so that his leg wound would not reopen.

"Well done of you, miss," Reed said.

"Well, I am a soldier's daughter, so in some ways nothing surprises me. If only the children are not harmed."

"We'll find them, miss. Don't you worry."

\*\*\*\*

Half an hour later Marian was pacing the drawing room, still in her bloody riding habit, as she told the magistrate all that Reed had said before the surgeon went to work on him. She'd made out some of the words he quoted. "Bordeaux" could have meant wine or the city.

Marian had never felt so helpless in her life. The magistrate promised to alert all his subordinates, but really there was very little they could do. The Watch was meant to patrol the streets, not find missing children. He advised her to hire someone from Bow Street. She was considering taking this measure without Wyle's consent. At least she would be doing something.

Her mother had invaded the kitchen to take charge, and they discovered that Reed was the Cook's nephew. Cook was coherent, but so many of the maids were weeping, and someone had to keep order. Mr. Hill was resting with a cold compress on his head and a footman in attendance, but he was still unconscious.

For the first time in many years Marian had an issue that required prayer, and yet she could not focus when she felt there was something she should be doing, something she had not thought of. If only she had possession of her fortune so she could help with the ransom, if indeed that was what the abductors wanted.

Frobisher wandered into the drawing room unannounced as though nothing untoward had happened. "Where's Wyle?" he asked Marian.

"Woolwich Academy, or he was. Didn't you see him there?"

"Nothing is happening there today."

"He went in response to your note."

"I sent nothing. We were supposed to lunch at White's today."

"Then who sent it?"

"Why is everyone below stairs wailing? Did someone die?"

"The children have been abducted and Hill and Reed both injured."

Frobisher staggered with alarm. "What? Where?"

"From Hyde Park."

He clutched his forehead. "But that's impossible. Who would do such a thing?"

"It *is* possible because it happened, but we have received no ransom demand as yet."

"This is terrible. I must find Wyle."

"He may be scouring the docks by now in case the abductors try to sail with them."

Frobisher spared her one anguished look before he strode from the room. Marian resumed her pacing, still convinced there was something else she should be doing if she could only think of it.

Hoby came back to report that Wyle was kicking up a dust in the port, threatening to search each ship personally if no one else would. Marian wrote him a brief note stating what little they knew. Reed had recalled some of the words but not understood them, so the only certain fact that could be established was that all the abductors were French. She sent Hoby off again with a brace of grooms in case Wyle needed them.

Trumby entered in Hoby's wake. "Miss, there is a gentleman here to see Captain Wyle, but he's the same one who called on you."

"Good Lord, what could Cole want? And at such a time! Show him into the breakfast parlor."

She waited a moment, then opened the door and found Cole staring at the family portrait over the fireplace. Henry must have been no more than two when it was painted. "What do you want now? I really cannot deal with you just now."

He started, then turned to her and drew himself to his full height. "I asked to see Captain Wyle."

"He is not home at the moment and I do not want you bothering him like you bothered my former employers."

"I came as soon as I heard."

"Heard what?" Marian snapped.

"That…that Lord Wyle's children have been abducted."

"I don't understand. How could you have heard?"

"It scarcely matters. Servants talk and news passes along the docks faster than through a ballroom. I have one of my yachts in port to take on war supplies. It is at Wyle's disposal since the cargo is not yet ready for shipment."

Marian recalled that Cole indeed owned several cargo vessels, but she felt so overwrought that she was ready to grasp at even this unwelcome aid. "He has not returned yet. The groom reports he is canvassing the docks. But we have no idea if the children have been carried out of the country."

"He can take one of my ships, the *Corunna*. It's small and can get into some ports not open to naval vessels. Or my crew can land him in a river mouth in a small boat."

"But where?" Marian pressed her fingertips to her temples for a moment. "Even if their French mother has had them abducted, we have no idea where she is."

"She is still with the Comte de Villars, as I recall. If Wyle finds them, I wager he will find the children."

"But he has no idea where Louisa is staying."

"Temporarily, at least, they are at Blaye, near the mouth of the Gironde River."

She felt herself gaping at him. "How could you possibly know this?"

"One of my duties for the government is to keep track of British and émigrés on the continent."

"You are a spy?" She took a step closer, staring at his face in disbelief.

Cole looked modest, a reach for him.

"I prefer the term 'intelligence officer.' "

"But why help us after all you have done to hinder me?"

"I admit I underestimated you. I thought you would concede that it is easier for me to handle your affairs than for you. Once we were locked in this battle…"

"Yes, your pride." Was he truly repentant?

"I will make it right with you. But that can wait.

Wyle must take this ship. It is his one chance to get into France incognito and recover his children."

"Cole, you are a good man after all." She felt overwhelmed by his generosity and embraced him.

The door opened and Wyle halted in his tracks. "Pardon me," he growled.

"Wyle, Cole has offered us one of his ships. And he knows the location of Louisa."

Wyle looked stunned. "But how?"

"I have connections in France. My mother was French. I have sometimes been able to get people out of France. As it happens, the Comte de Villars contacted my French agent seeking passage out of France for his wife."

"And you refused?"

"Yes, since Villars is also a Captain of Horse in Napoleon's army, I sensed a trap. I suspect the upshot is they have abducted the children so they can take them to another country."

Wyle shook his head. "Why, after all this time?"

"Please accept my help. I feel partly responsible for this situation. By refusing to give her passage, I may have provoked the abduction."

Wyle still looked puzzled. "No, you cannot be held to blame. You did the right thing."

"I offer my ship, the *Corunna*, to carry you across. It can wait offshore until you find them."

"When can I leave?" Wyle demanded.

"On the next tide, if you wish."

"I'll pack," Marian said.

"You are not going," Wyle said flatly.

"Why not?" asked Cole. "She will be perfectly safe on the ship."

"An unmarried lady on a commercial vessel without

accompaniment in a time of war? Need I say more? I must go and make arrangements for the ransom in case we have guessed wrongly and it is needed here."

Marian bit her lower lip. "Perhaps Wyle is right. Someone must be here in case a ransom demand comes."

"It's a good thing I planned to resign my commission. I must be at liberty to search for the children."

Cole glanced at him. "As a British officer you would be safer in France than as a private citizen."

"Perhaps. I must give orders, and I have some other documents to prepare." Wyle left them without even looking back. Marian felt abandoned.

"I cannot stand here doing nothing," she said.

"I know you. I will send my carriage in the early morning, well before we sail. If you wish to go, it should be your choice, not Wyle's. The girl especially may have need of you."

"Yes, of course. I will watch for the carriage. And I'll be discreet when I get to the ship."

"Good. I will keep Wyle busy. Do not bring a ton of baggage."

She just looked at him.

"No, of course you would not. Until then." Cole kissed her hand. It was the first time she had thought of him in a companionable way, as though he was useful instead of an obstruction. Had she misjudged him?

She saw him out of the house and watched through the hall window as he mounted his horse and galloped off. She had just turned to go up the stairs to pack a small valise when the front door opened and a very grubby Henry staggered in.

"Oh, Henry! Are you all right? What happened?"

She ran to him so fast she nearly fell.

"They've taken Charlotte, and it took me all this time to make my way home. Catch me going about without fare for a hack again."

"Trumby, tell Lord Wyle that Henry is back."

"They've taken her to an inn. I saw the name of it. *The Pelican*," he gasped, then sat on the floor in exhaustion.

Wyle almost fell as he loped down the stairs to clutch Henry in his arms. "Are you indeed unharmed?"

Marian could see the tears in Wyle's eyes. Henry began to cry as well but sniffed and looked up. "Charlotte helped me get away. She kicked one of the men in the carriage, then bit the other one and told me to run. I hopped out and hid in a milk cart until I could get my hands free. Did my horse come home?"

"Yes, he's fine. Where did they take her?"

"We were south of the river in a very nasty part of town. It stank of fish."

"Tell me how you came home."

"I saw a sign that said *Pelican Inn*. I ran for half an hour before I came to Blackfriars Bridge."

"You did well, Henry. Now rest, and the surgeon will look at you. Trumby, have four horses saddled and tell three of the grooms we have an errand. I want them armed."

"Be careful," was all Marian said before she helped Henry to his feet and to the kitchen. If she guessed aright, a meal was what he needed. A good sleep would come soon enough.

Chapter Twelve

It seemed as though Wyle had been gone for hours. Henry was asleep after telling his tale to the magistrate, whom they had summoned again. Blessedly, Hill was awake, though he did not remember the attack at all. He was trying to get up, and it was all Marian could do to dissuade him. Leaving a footman to restrain him and also get some food into him, she was pacing the drawing room, a lamentable habit but better than doing nothing.

Wyle thundered into the courtyard with his grooms but no Charlotte. A moment later he entered and threw off his cloak. "Is Hill coherent yet? And can you rouse your mother and Cook and bring them to the drawing room?"

She felt a shiver, but her mind leaped immediately to match the people he requested with his mission. "A marriage license?"

"Easy enough to obtain these days."

"Well, time is short. But Mr. Hill must not leave his bed."

"Very well, we shall go to him."

Marian returned a few minutes later with the other two women, and now Wyle seemed to hesitate. "There should be flowers or something."

"There will be later. For now we must find Charlotte. Your promise is enough."

She gripped his hand and found it cold but strong,

so they went up the stairs to Hill's room.

"It seems fantastic that you should be sailing off to France and on one of Cole's ships. Do you really believe Louisa has done this thing?"

"All evidence points to it. Besides, we have received no ransom demand. If we do, then you have the power to act for me, but only as my wife."

When Wyle explained their errand, Hill looked confused. "You want me to marry you? From my bed?"

"Is there any rule against it?"

"None that I know of. This means you have not found Charlotte and mean to go after her into France."

"I want to leave Marian in charge as my wife, a stronger position than as my fiancée. I have brought your *Book of Common Prayer*."

"Very well, may I at least stand?"

"If you think you can."

Hill struggled into a robe and stood, swaying only slightly. He then read the words that would bind Marian to her fate. Wyle's kiss at the end was chaste, and they left Hill to go back to sleep. Wyle went to the library to plan his passage. Cole was back by then with French maps and harbor charts.

By tomorrow, Wyle would be on his way to France and she would either be here pacing or be stowed in a cabin waiting to surprise and defy him. For once, the choice was hers. How ironic that it was Cole who gave her that choice.

****

Marian fell into a fitful sleep but awoke after a few hours, upbraiding herself yet again for not riding with the children. If she had been along…what? Would she have been able to prevent the abduction? She did not normally ride armed except for the boot dirk her father had given her. And not even Wyle had foreseen the possibility of the kidnapping.

And that was the strangest part of the whole misadventure. If it was someone seeking ransom, they would have sent a note by now. If it was his wife wanting to hurt Wyle, would she have terrified her own children in the process? It made no sense.

Unless the villain was not Louisa. Perhaps Isabelle's early morning visit was more than an accident. What if she was there to distract her and Wyle from the children? But what motive could she have other than her jealousy? Surely even the vicious Isabelle wouldn't risk the lives of Wyle's children just to show Marian up as incompetent. And she could not hope to carry out a ransom scheme.

Marian shook her head. Fatigue and stress were making her irrational. She just had to sleep. At least they had gotten a start on the rescue, with Cole's help. He had found out about the abduction very quickly. They were lucky to have his aid, though it seemed overly convenient. Perhaps he was just more a man of action than she had supposed. When he had returned, he had already made preparations for Wyle's rescue mission and Wyle had agreed to them.

Cole's claim that he had heard of the abduction via gossip seemed strange. Though Wyle had made a stink at the harbor, that was among the officials, and his servants did not gossip. Even if they did, there would have been no time.

What was the point of going over it again and again in her head when they knew so little? She feared for more than Charlotte's life. If those rough men hurt her in any way, she would take a pistol to them herself. Why? Why would her mother send creatures like that who were sure to terrify Charlotte? Marian could only picture the girl, bound, without a decent change of clothes.

If only Wyle had not been called away. But if Frobisher had not sent the note, who had? Clearly someone who knew Wyle's circumstances with the army, plus when and where they rode.

The blood froze in her veins and she sat bolt upright. Cole. If he was able to get detailed information on Louisa, then finding out about Wyle would be no challenge. But if he needed money, why not complete the ransom? Because he wanted something else. Then it hit her that if not for Isabelle, Marian would have been with the children.

Cole wanted Marian. She already knew that it was a matter of pride. She considered the possibility that if she had been in the park the children would not have been taken. But Cole knew he could never compel her to marriage without the children as hostages. Yes, she would do anything to protect them. Besides, he'd sent half a dozen men. They had meant to take all three of them.

Cole *had* been surprised when she walked into the drawing room. He had asked for Wyle because he assumed Marian was tied up in a carriage somewhere, possibly aboard one of his ships by now. So he had meant to trap Wyle as well, not just coerce her into marriage but possibly have his revenge on the man who loved her. It was her fault Charlotte was in danger and Wyle was being led into a trap. How could she tell him that? If she told him, would he even believe her?

She rose and dressed, then loaded a brace of pistols,

packed a few clothes, and penned a document that might make up for her dereliction. The adjoining door opened and her mother came through in her dressing gown.

"What are you doing?"

"Writing you a power of attorney that will put you in control of Henry and of Wyle's affairs until we return. Then I am packing. I sail with Wyle. I have prepared my will also."

"I suspected as much. Marian, are you sure you should do this?"

"Cole said it. She will need me more than her father when we find her."

"And I must risk you."

"It's not in me to sit idly by."

"I would come too."

"We need someone here to pay the ransom if a ransom is requested, and to take care of Henry."

"Why would it not be requested? I live in momentary expectation of us being contacted, yet all of you are sailing off to France."

"If it is their mother, she wants her children, not money."

"But she is dead."

"She is with her husband. The marriage to Wyle was not legal."

Her mother looked confused. "And if it is not her, who is it?"

Marian wanted to spare her mother as much worry as possible. "I don't know who else would have a reason to think Wyle is that wealthy."

"Still, the poorest would envy his competence."

Marian put on her cloak. "There is no point in disputing."

"Go if you mean to go. Is Wyle coming for you?"

"He—a carriage is being sent. I must be ready." She hugged her mother, handed her the documents, then made for the back stairs with her valise. There she found Hill fully dressed but still looking like death warmed over.

"The carriage waiting in the stable yard—is that for you?"

"Yes."

"I am coming with you."

"With your head? You might keel over at any moment and die."

"Don't you understand?" He licked his dry lips and put a far from steady hand on her arm. "If Charlotte is harmed or killed, I don't care what happens to me. If you don't let me come, I will find a way."

"I cannot say I blame you. Here is one of my father's old pistols. Keep it by you. I have the other."

As they got into the carriage, she questioned her choice of dress, her riding habit from which she'd blotted out the blood. But there might be a need for horses. The pocket of her old gray cloak held her loaded pistol and her boot a dagger. The small bag contained a change of shirt and a dress for Charlotte if—no, when—they found her.

She thought of the girl as she had last seen her and tried to project caring thoughts Charlotte's way. If she was right about Cole, then not only had Wyle walked into his trap but she was doing so as well, and she was taking poor Hill along with her. But it was too late now to take any precautions against the fate that might await her. And even if she knew for certain, she had no choice but to go.

Before they reached the ship, she decided she had to

apprise Hill of her suspicions.

"I have been thinking about the false message we got that sent Wyle haring off to Woolwich."

"Yes, they thought me no danger, and they were right."

"I think the plan was to abduct me as well."

Hill stared at her. "To take care of them, you mean?"

"No. My cousin wants me. I'm assuming he is having trouble taking over father's estate without me as his wife. So his intent may be marriage."

"But you refused him."

"And since Wyle informed him we are engaged, that may have driven him to desperation."

Hill stared out the window into the darkness. "It makes sense."

"So if you do not want to go…"

"Not go? Do you think I care if it's a trap?"

"No I expected you wouldn't. You do believe me? You don't think it's a fantastical imagining?"

"It also explains how your cousin knows so much so early."

"Yes, but will Wyle grasp the plot?" Marian asked.

"Sometimes, if it's not his idea, he can be critical of it."

"Louisa is still alive."

"I have always known that, but I doubt she has any part in this plot."

When they reached the dock, a boat was waiting. Cole's ship was not at the dock but sat off in the Thames waiting for cargo. They were rowed out to the *Corunna*. Her cousin was waiting on deck. "Good, you made haste. Who is with you?"

"A groom. We may have need of a messenger who

can ride."

"Wyle is below, and I will keep him there until we are past the point of returning."

"We will wait up here."

"Do not fall overboard. No, you wouldn't." He left them sitting in the lee of the cabin on a crate.

"Why did you conceal my identity?" Hill whispered.

"I don't want Cole to count you as a threat to his plot. Go to the other end of the ship and keep your ears open. The seamen will not be expecting an English groom to know any French."

Hill nodded and made his way forward, staggering either from the wash of the retreating tide or his lightheadedness.

She could hear their voices in the cabin below, Wyle's steady rumble in spite of his stress and Cole's hissing whisper as though he were a conspirator. Finally, long after the sails were unfurled and they were rolling across the waves, Hill returned to sit on the crate and cradle his aching head. They might be two days at sea if the wind was against them, but it seemed to be driving them southeast, which was where they wanted to go. She cringed as boot steps sounded on the companionway.

When he finally left off planning and came on deck, Wyle paid scant attention to the two sailors malingering by the aft cabin until he noted the tiny size of the booted feet of one of them. He looked further in the dim light of the stern lantern and made out a gray cloak. "Oh, no. Marian, is that you?"

"Of course it's me." She stood but did not pull Hill to his feet.

"But why? Why put yourself in danger when I need you at home?"

"I have given my mother a power of attorney to act for me. You're not the only one who can write documents."

"I know, and I suppose she can pay the ransom as easily as you can, but I did not want you with me. By God. Hill, is that you?"

"Quiet. Cole thinks he's a groom."

"What game are you two playing?"

"After all your talk about courage," she hissed. "Was that just lip service to get me to the altar? Did you mean none of it?"

"Courage is situational. It takes a great deal more to wait patiently at home than to actually go out and face the unknown."

"Ah, then I am a coward after all. Indeed I could not bear to wait for you."

"I want both of you to stay on the ship. They will land me in the mouth of the Gironde River in a small boat and wait for me to return with Charlotte."

"No, nothing would be more fatal. Neither of you would return."

"If I am discovered, you can escape. Your cousin will help you try again."

"Yes, Cole. I don't suppose he is going upriver with you."

"It's not his place to go."

"And what if Charlotte is not with Louisa?" she asked.

"She must be. Who else would want her?"

Marian gripped the rail. "What if you don't find her there? Possibly you will be captured by the French, if they have been alerted."

"Who would alert the French? I return and seek

155

intelligence elsewhere."

"And if the ship is gone?" Hill whispered.

Wyle spun toward him. "Why would it be gone?"

"Has Louisa ever asked for the children before?" Hill rubbed his forehead.

"Yes, before she faked her death, but we've been at war. There was no chance she could force me to surrender them. Charlotte must be with her. Who else would want to steal her?"

Marian blew out a tired breath. "Well I had thought of Isabelle."

Wyle's laugh was a dry cackle. "You can't be serious. She can't plot her way out of a garden, and why would she?"

"I too discarded that idea." Marian cleared her throat. "When a problem seems insoluble, my father always said, turn it on its head."

"What are you talking about?"

"Did you get to talk to Frobisher before we left?"

"No, we were to lunch at White's. I didn't even think to send him a note. I suppose he'll hear it from the servants."

"Frobisher came to the house and I told him. He did not send the message that called you to Woolwich."

"That's strange. No one knew what I was talking about when I arrived."

"Someone did not want you riding with us," Hill said.

Wyle stared at them.

Hill stepped closer. "Someone who has made a point of discovering your circumstances and Louisa's. Who knows the fact that she is not dead but with her original husband."

"Greenway? This is a fantastic accusation. He is helping us find them. And why would he do this?"

"If not for Isabelle, I would have been riding with them," Marian reminded him.

"Are you saying he meant to abduct you?"

"All of us. The children to compel me to marry him."

Wyle shuddered. "And it would have worked. You would have sacrificed yourself to save them."

"Of course."

"But what would he have done with them? They could identify him."

"I don't know. I can only hope he would have let them go."

"Didn't his offer of help come out of the blue so quickly we jumped at it?" Hill asked.

Wyle stared at both of them. "But if you knew it was Cole, why did you come?"

"To warn you, of course," Marian said desperately.

"Would you two keep your voices down?" Hill whispered fiercely. "Some of these scum do know a bit of English."

"Cole knew about the abduction before it could have been common knowledge."

Wyle staggered against the rail. "But why take you to France?"

"I don't know why he would need to get me out of England in his power. But maybe we are only going to France because he now has Charlotte and can lure you there and have you killed. I don't imagine he cares whether you see your daughter again or not."

"If I'm dead, he figures your mother won't fight him for the estate. Are you sure?"

"That's the hell of it," Marian said. "We cannot be sure. So we have to pretend that he is helping us. Once we land, we may well be safer to stay in France. Our troops cannot be so far from the border now."

"True." Wyle sighed. "And what if Charlotte is not with Louisa, and Cole doesn't have her either?"

"Then we go back and wait." Marian stared at the rolling sea. "Our choices are limited. But since this way has been made so smooth for us, I'm inclined to think Cole has hired a house somewhere in the neighborhood where Villars lives, planning for you to be conveniently ambushed."

"If I knew for certain, I would smash his teeth down his throat."

"Not until he leads us to where she is. You are cold under fire, and you are going to have to be very cool if you want to save her life."

"And yours," Wyle added.

"I do not imagine mine is in any danger. But one word about our marriage would put a period to your existence, so be careful what you say."

He stared at her. "Did you always plan to go, or only after you realized you were stepping into a trap?"

"It's only a trap if we don't know about it," Hill whispered.

"What a pair you are." He wanted to embrace Marian, which would have been fine in front of Hill but not of the crew who all reported to Greenway.

"He wants you," Wyle whispered. "I can see it in his eyes."

"But why? I have never given him any encouragement. My fortune is nothing compared to what he has made running French brandy into the country."

"I had thought him a legitimate shipper."

"I would not put it past him to sell our arms to the enemy if he could get away with it."

"What?"

"Father always suspected the smuggling trade was the source of Cole's wealth, which is why we so seldom visited his house. He flaunted the signs of it too obviously—the best brandy, the paintings, gilt furnishings."

"Then he wants you for the respectability you would bring him, besides your father's property."

"I had not thought of that. So it must pain him to think of me as a governess."

"I swear, if he is responsible for terrifying and endangering my child, I will kill him."

"In good time. For now, we have no choice but to let him lead us to her."

"And no one to help us if things go awry."

"Hill will be useful in a scrape. He has a pistol. So do I."

Wyle glanced at Hill, who had sat down again and seemed to have fallen asleep. "He is as tenacious as a terrier. It gets better and better. The three of us against a crew of thirty-odd sailors. Why was I worried?"

"That's the spirit. When do we reach the Gironde?"

"At this speed, before dawn tomorrow. You need to get some sleep."

"I could not. Don't you see? This is all my fault. If not for me, Charlotte would be perfectly safe."

His scarred hand reached for hers, picked it up, and pressed it to his lips. "You are not to be thinking that. You are not at all responsible for your disreputable cousin's machinations."

"If he has hurt her, I will kill him myself."
"You may have to fight me for the privilege."

## Chapter Thirteen

When Marian awoke, she was nestled among the extra sails in the locker. Wyle was sitting beside her looking at the ocean.

"What time do you make it to be?" she asked.

"Nearly noon by the bells. We should be anchoring soon."

She sat up and gave a sigh. "Will you miss it? Soldiering?"

She could see his mouth twist into a wry smile. "Not now that my private life is fraught with danger."

"That was an unkind question."

"But a valid one. Your cousin advised me not to resign since I would be safer as a soldier than as a private citizen."

"That isn't true, is it?"

"No, if he turns me in, I'll be imprisoned if I'm in uniform. If he induces me to dress as a civilian, I'd be hung as a spy without a trial."

"Then we must keep an eye on him."

A boy appeared then with mugs of tea on a tray and some slices of coarse buttered bread.

"I'd better wake Hill if I can."

"He's already about," Wyle said.

Hill made his way back to them.

"You seem to have found your sea legs," Marian observed.

"The pitching in my head is canceled out by the roll of the ship. They are going to wait offshore till nightfall and run into the river under cover of darkness, then put us off in a small boat."

Wyle blew out a tired breath. "We have to wait, the hardest part. I have plenty of gold French coin for a carriage or horses, whatever we can get. No one utter a word of English after we disembark."

"*Oui*," Marian agreed.

\*\*\*\*

Marian occupied the time with examining in turn all the things that could still go wrong at this point. She had a plan, to be sure, but one she could not divulge to either Wyle or Hill until it was time. Once they had Charlotte, she could only hope they would trust her to take care of matters. Hill might. But Wyle in so many ways was still an unknown entity. He was too much like her. He was the one who always wanted to make everything safe. He would never trust her to handle anything, but if he had to choose between saving her or his daughter, she prayed he would save Charlotte.

They sailed as far up the Gironde as was navigable, past at least one town, for she saw the lights. The longboat would have to be rowed against the tide. The *Corunna* would drift back to the ocean to wait off Pointe de Grave for them.

When the boat was lowered, Wyle and Hill went down after the two oarsmen were in place. Marian followed.

"You must not go," Cole said when Marian descended the rope ladder to the ship's longboat.

"You convinced me I must. As you said, she will need me when we find her."

"But this is France."

"And I speak French better than any of you, including your crew, so let us stop arguing and debark."

Cole finally followed her down to the boat, though she doubted he had planned to do so before she showed her determination. Besides Hill, there were five crewmen. That brought the odds to two to one. She smiled and Wyle must have read her thoughts for he nodded his approval.

An hour later they landed at a waterfront town, Blaye, she supposed, which boasted an inn. They left two men with the boat while Marian dickered for the price of a carriage and team.

Cole paid the innkeeper with a gold Louis coin. Wyle tried not to notice this, but it would have been obvious not to remark on it.

"These were minted in Belgium," Cole said, "and captured by British forces. How nice to be able to trade with the enemy in their own coin."

She was not happy three of the crew accompanied them. And she made Hill's seasickness an excuse for him riding inside where nothing could happen to him. He wisely kept his hat on and his head down.

"Have you ever been to this house before?" Cole asked.

"No, how could I?" Wyle asked. "I have not seen Charlotte's mother in years."

Cole rubbed his large chin. "Perhaps we should try a clandestine approach."

"No," Marian said. "I will go to the door. The two of you will stand to each side. When they let me in, you will crowd after me."

"All of us?" Wyle asked.

"No, only you two and Hill. We do not want the world to know our errand. I trust you have been discreet with what you told your men, Cole."

"Of course," he said, scrutinizing Hill. "I suppose your groom is to be trusted."

"Implicitly," Wyle said.

Marian had rehearsed her speech. She would tell the servant she had information touching on the children. Even if Charlotte was held here, she thought she would be admitted.

The house was a small stone structure of two floors, fronting close on the road. The carriage barely had space to pull off the way. It went better than expected. The feeble retainer backed away, bowing and making no attempt to block the path of Wyle, Cole, or Hill. He showed them into a salon where a fragile blonde woman sat beside a weary man in a French dragoon's uniform. When he perceived Wyle's coat, he drew his sword left-handed, with a gasp of pain. "You are English."

"Yes, as it happens," Wyle said.

The man staggered to his feet and took a protective stance in front of the woman. "Then we are indeed overrun, and without warning."

"Not yet." Wyle had not drawn his weapon, though Cole was holding a pistol. "Please put your weapon down, Greenway. Louisa, I am searching for Charlotte."

"Searching?" The woman rose and tottered. "Do you mean she has run away?"

"No, she has been abducted."

"*Mon Dieu*." The count dropped his saber and went to take Louisa's hand and comfort her, though at the moment he looked paler than she did.

"No one has contacted us for ransom," Louisa said.

Marian noted that the man's green uniform had been patched in several places, and the rest of the poor furnishings suggested they were impoverished.

"Louisa, I think he means he suspects we have abducted her."

"That is absurd. I would love to see my Charlotte, but I would never endanger her. We are about to be overrun by the British army."

The French officer turned back to them. "As you have surmised, I am le comte de Villars. Since I am on leave, I had some thought of taking Louisa out of the path of danger. We have, in fact, made contact with a packet that may take her to England incognito. Will I be arrested?"

"Not by me. As you've probably guessed, I am Lord Wyle. I'm interested only in getting Charlotte back."

Cole cocked the pistol. "You believe them? I thought you would have been outraged, demanded an explanation from them."

"Put that away," Wyle said. "Someone could accidentally be shot in a disturbance. No, I believe them, but it does leave us at trail's end, so to speak."

Cole did take the hammer off cock and seemed to be thinking. "If the abductor was going to demand a ransom from the mother, they would be holding the girl in this area. I shall send my men to the local tavern and see what they can discover."

"Oh, please do," Louisa said. "Whatever they ask, I will pay it."

The count opened his mouth to say something, then closed it with a sad smile. "Whatever we have can be used for the ransom. There are always your jewels."

"Yes, take them. We must get her back."

Marian had wondered how she would feel about Louisa, but she felt only sadness for her. "Perhaps we should not impose on the count and his lady any longer."

The man's fair hair fell across his still handsome but worn face. Only his brown eyes held some energy. "I'm sorry. You are?"

"Miss Greenway, the governess."

The count raised an eyebrow, but Louisa accepted the explanation.

"If only we knew who did this," Louisa said, then began weeping. Her husband put his handkerchief in her hand.

The count rang then for the aged servant and invited the party to supper, such as it was. Marian was thankful for the hot soup, bread, and reviving wine. Louisa had many questions about Henry and Charlotte. Wyle answered each patiently. She held a locket with the two of them in it, old pictures. Marian found herself much in sympathy with the woman and vowed to send new portraits of the children. But for the moment they had to wait on the whim of Cole.

Sure enough, his men returned with *rumors* of an English girl being held an hour's drive away by coach.

After he gave them directions, Villars said, "I know this place. It is little more than a ruin. I will have my horse saddled and come with you. You may need safe conduct through the region."

"We appreciate the offer, but it's full night now. No one is likely to accost us. Besides, someone must stay with Louisa."

"Perhaps Miss Greenway."

"No, Charlotte will need me when we find her. I must go."

Louisa burst into tears again, so the count was prevailed on to stay with his wife.

Wyle turned at the door. "I will bring Charlotte back for a visit before taking her home."

"Is there nothing we can do?" Villars asked.

"The hardest task of all—wait."

In just less than an hour, they stopped the coach at a turn in the drive at their destination, out of sight of the front gate. Marian jumped out and the others followed. The chateau, as the count had said, was little more than a ruin. Wyle would have been surprised if there was a sound roof among all the buildings. "How shall we approach this time, Marian?" Cole asked. "Rap on the door?"

"No, I think stealth is in order this time. I promised the coachman a fortune to wait for us. I suggest you and the rest of your men scale that wall to the left while we slip in through some break in the ruin on the right. There is sure to be one."

"I perceive you assign us the more strenuous task. I don't know why I let you have the ordering of this expedition."

Nevertheless he went off with the seamen while Wyle led Marian and Hill around the upended building blocks and fallen walls by the easiest path.

"Will they scale the wall, do you think?" Wyle asked.

"Not if one of his henchmen is on the alert for them," Marian said. "It serves the purpose of separating them from us."

"Wonderful. They will be waiting inside," Wyle said.

"But we know it. I assure you I have a plan. I suggest

starting our search in the basement of the main house."

"The donjon," Hill quipped. "Better and better."

The iron fence that bordered the property along the steep hillside was contorted by some tree roots enough for them to slip through. They found an opening into the house near the middle of the back wall at what used to be a stairway into the yard.

"I had forgotten we might need a light," Wyle whispered.

"Nothing would be more fatal. We can feel our way to a door that goes upstairs."

Along the main corridor of the basement there was already a dim light burning off to one side. They crept along the hall, and Wyle stood on his toes to look into the barred grill. "My God! It's Major Greenway."

"Who's there?" the man whispered.

"Papa, are you indeed there? Are you all right?"

"Marian, I should have known. The key is on the ledge over the door. They have not brought my supper yet, so you must be quick."

Hill found the key and finessed the lock. Wyle eased the door open with an effort, and Marian embraced her father.

"Did you know he might be here?" Wyle asked in amazement.

"I had some faint hope."

"Sir, you must make your way out and wait for us," Hill said. "We have still to rescue Wyle's daughter."

"The girl I heard crying? I'm coming with you."

"In that case, which is the way to the stair?"

"Follow me." He picked up the stump of candle and led them forward into the gloom.

"You move well for a man held in a damp

basement."

"Up until yesterday I was kept prisoner outside Bordeaux. Why they moved me here I have no idea."

"Cole was drawing everyone together," Marian said. "He knew where Louisa was because the count made contact to get them out of France, so he had Charlotte brought here, and you as well."

"To what purpose?" her father asked.

"Of that I am not sure. I think his machinations included only you and me until I became engaged to Wyle. Now I think he wants both of you dead. Charlotte's capture was to compel my compliance."

"I would have come for you if he had taken you," Wyle assured her.

"Perhaps that's what he had in mind, a handy trap to get you here, then his revenge."

They crept up the stairs and found the basement door gave onto the kitchen. Though there were food smells, no one was about, so they picked up extra weapons and crept toward the door. It was ajar, and by peeking through the crack Wyle could see Charlotte at one end of the table staring at her plate.

"You must eat, my dear," Cole said. "How else will you keep up your strength?"

"Why have you done this?"

"No appetite, I see. Perhaps if the rest of our guests join us," he said with a raised voice. A man out of sight to the right of the door pushed it open, and Wyle had no choice but to step into the room. Besides the sailors, there were half a dozen other men around the periphery, counting the cook.

"Father!" Charlotte bolted from the table and fell into his arms.

"Has he hurt you?"

"No, but he frightened me. Why did he take us, and what happened to Henry?"

"Henry is fine. As to why, I imagine it was to get me here. You see he wants to marry your dear governess, and I seem to be an impediment to his plans."

"Miss Greenway! You're here as well? And Mr. Hill." Charlotte left her father's arms to fall into Hill's.

"And me, Miss Greenway's father. At one point Cousin Cole thought my imprisonment would compel my daughter into marriage. Had she agreed to such a match, my life would have been worth nothing."

"As opposed to now?" Cole asked.

"He thinks he has found a better lever," Hill snarled, "an innocent child."

Cole stood. "You men, take them all below except Miss Greenway."

"You scum," Hill shouted and drew his sword on the two men who approached with cutlasses.

"No!" Marian yelled.

Wyle found himself facing Cole and hoped Marian would have enough sense to get Charlotte out of harm's way. He could see Major Greenway fending off two of the ruffians with an iron candle stand and Marian laying about her with a large frying pan she'd grabbed from the table. It looked hot, the contents having scalded one of her opponents.

For a large man, Cole fenced well, better than a maimed soldier. Wyle kicked a chair in front of him but only tripped the cook, who was trying to escape the room. Cole bore down on him and knocked him onto the table. He rolled over it backward but landed badly on his game leg. Cole grinned and raised his saber to strike.

A pistol report filled the room with smoke and noise. Everyone hesitated, and Cole dropped his sword with a grimace. "You nearly took my hand off. You'll pay for that."

"Just evening the odds," Marian said. "Now that I have your attention, swordplay was never on the agenda for this meeting."

"It wasn't?" Wyle asked.

"No, we came to negotiate."

Cole smirked. "With what? You haven't even a shot left. Seeing that you have no leverage…" He sneered as Marian approached, her hand beside her skirt.

"You'll listen to me or you'll be picking your guts up off this floor. A knife is always loaded."

Major Greenway chuckled as Cole turned pale, staring down at the blade pressing at his ample belly.

"Now that I have your attention, here are my terms. Everyone gets to leave unmolested and I stay, provided you are willing to marry me."

A chorus of "No!" met her statement, but Cole glanced shrewdly at her. "I could have them all killed and have you anyway."

"Might I remind you how much more pleasant a willing wife would be?"

"That was your plan?" Wyle asked in horror. "To stay with him?"

"You never trusted me, Wyle," Marian said. "A grave mistake on your part."

He looked at her with such pain in his eyes. Would he understand finally that she could take care of herself? If not, if he tried to play the hero in this, they might all die. Finally he seemed to come to a decision and stared at her with a pleading look that said better than words,

*Please keep safe.*

"What do I get out of this besides you?" Cole asked. "You're not much of a bargain."

Marian looked up at Cole. "I guarantee you freedom from prosecution. If they send the law after you, I die. And they don't want the scandal anyway. Father's estate will come to you in time through me. Not as quickly as you had hoped, but you have enough put by to survive. Smuggling will be harder once the war is over and the navy can be employed to keep it in check. Besides, I have the one thing you have always found out of reach."

"What is that?"

"Respectability."

He gave a short laugh and looked down. "That sounds odd coming from a woman holding a knife to someone's gut."

"Nevertheless, that is all I am prepared to offer. And it is your gut."

He snorted a laugh. "I see your point. Agreed."

"I have to see them all leave and all your men will wait inside with us to assure me they are not followed."

"Father!" Charlotte shouted. "You cannot allow this!"

"I don't think Miss Greenway is giving any of us much choice. What say you, Major?"

"There's no reasoning with Marian when she is like this. I recommend we obey her orders."

"But, sir…" Hill protested. He pressed his hand over an arm wound bleeding sluggishly, which Charlotte finally noticed and attempted to stanch with her scrap of handkerchief.

"I had the carriage brought into the courtyard," Cole said. "Be gone in five minutes."

"Come, all of you," the major ordered, as he picked up a saber in place of the candlestand.

Marian walked with her cousin to the window to watch. Hill untied the wizened coachman, but it was Wyle who drove, with the terrified Frenchman up beside him pointing the way. As the carriage disappeared, she felt satisfaction. She was far from safe herself, but at least everyone else was.

"The wedding will have to wait," Cole said. "English clergymen don't grow on trees in France."

"No, I don't expect they do. Have you a chamber where I can wash up?"

"Wash up? First give me that pig sticker."

"You may have it now."

"You." He pointed the knife at the cook. "Hot water to my chamber. Now."

Then he took Marian's arm and escorted her upstairs. There was rubble on the steps from the roof, and the boards of the upstairs hall were uneven, but he thrust open the door to a chamber that seemed to have been preserved. At least the bed hangings were not rotten and the furniture unbroken.

"I have waited a long time for this," he said, standing back to look at her.

"Is there any wine? Perhaps brandy."

"No, we don't want any wine. Next you'll be ordering tea as though this is all normal when it is not." His hand clenched on the knife did not disturb her. After he had fought so hard to get her here, she did not think he would kill her.

"Cole, the whole situation is of your making. It turned out as you planned. How is that not normal?"

He opened his mouth to reply, but the cook slid in

with a pannikin of steaming water. Marian discarded her cloak and jacket, then unbuttoned her cuffs and picked up the soap. "Mmm, French. No one can make soap like the French."

"I must be going mad. Is this all it took to win you, an abduction?"

"Well, I suppose your plan was not so convoluted. You planned to have them snatch me along with the children. But the deal would still have been the same. If you had killed my father, I would have hunted you down like a cur." She dried her face and hands, then glanced around the room.

"You set a pretty high price on yourself. I hope you're worth it."

"You're the one who set the price. Just remember that." She walked to the bureau. "Ah, brandy."

"If you're thinking to get me drunk, it won't work. I have a hard head."

"No, I'm thinking to get *me* drunk. I don't want to remember any of this. I need a glass."

He turned impatiently to pick up a glass from the bedside table and the decanter crashed into his skull and took him down. Marian bolted the door, gagged him, and began the arduous task of tying him up with strips of bed linen.

****

"You are going back for her, aren't you?" Charlotte called from inside the coach.

"Don't worry," Major Greenway assured her. "You don't imagine that is the only knife she has. It was a kitchen knife, so she still has her boot dirk I gave her, hidden away."

"I'm going back as soon as we reach the road," Wyle

174

said. "Hill can't drive with that arm. The coachman is too distraught. What about you, Major Greenway? I'll go back in the way we did before—"

"No, there is another door," Greenway said, craning his neck out the window.

"I'm coming too," Hill said.

"Arrgh, we all just escaped. We can't all go back. Hill, you have to take care of Charlotte. The major and I can handle this."

"I think I can manage it alone," Greenway said.

A group of three horsemen confronted the carriage, and Wyle had no choice but to stop. If they were highwaymen...

"*C'est moi*, le comte de Villars."

"Sir, you should not be on a horse," Wyle said.

"Charlotte, is she with you?"

"Yes, and she is fine. This solves our problem. Villars, can you lend us your horses and take Charlotte and Hill home in the carriage?"

"I know I am not much use, but I should be helping you."

"Making sure Charlotte is safe will be help enough. We have to go back for Marian, hence the need for the horses."

"They are yours." The count dismounted with a hop and ordered his servants to take charge of the carriage while he limped to the door and got inside with Charlotte and Hill.

They made the exchange and cantered back, surprised to find the main gate still open. They tethered the horses and were making their way toward the side door and discussing their entry when a large bundle slid out of an upper window and inched down the side of the building on silken bed cords, then tied-together sheets, which apparently fell short of the distance, for the bundle dropped the last ten feet with a thud.

"Is that your nephew?" Wyle asked as the major started to chuckle.

Marian's head appeared in the window. "Yes, we may need him," she whispered.

"But you've used up all the rope," Wyle complained. "How will you get down?"

"On this vine. It will support my weight."

Not to Wyle's surprise, Marian had secreted breeches under her riding dress and now tossed her skirt and cloak down in a bundle. She found toe and handholds on the ivy, but half a story from the bottom it pulled away from the stones and Wyle rushed forward and caught her.

"Is everything going according to your plan now?" he asked, setting her on her feet.

"Except the need for conveyance."

"We have managed to borrow three horses from the count."

"Well, we could use four, but I suppose three is better than none."

Wyle blew out a breath. "Had I known you meant to capture prisoners, I'd have taken that into account."

Marian glared at them. "Do I have to do everything myself? Is there nothing in the stable? I'll go look."

"I'll go," her father said. "I thought I heard old Becket trumpeting."

They occupied themselves with carrying Cole to the horses. Between them they were able to heave him up onto the back of the sturdiest beast and tie him in place. Wyle wondered how Marian had dragged the big man to the window and pushed him out, not to mention lowering him to the ground. She must be exhausted.

"A half hitch around a sturdy bedpost, in case you are wondering."

They were both breathless, but Wyle chuckled and hugged her to his chest. "With a bit of luck we might just get away."

The major returned, mounted. "Look, they did bring Becket with them. He's a little underfed but eager for action."

Marian mounted the smallest horse. "Good, now we must get our party together at the count's house."

"Won't these fellows miss their leader?" Wyle asked.

"If I mistake not, they are three parts drunk already and assuming Cole won't be down till morning. Still, it might be best to take ship before dawn, if possible."

"Is she always like this, so managing?" Wyle asked the major.

"Only when at war. It's like she has two people bottled up inside her."

"Yes, I've met the prim one, and she is formidable as well."

"You'd think the prim and proper one would not let her fling her reputation away on a rescue in a foreign country," her father quipped.

"My reputation?"

"Coming to France without a chaperone. Or at least I hope your mother is not lurking about somewhere." Major Greenway made a show of looking out through the trees.

"Lurking? No, she is holding the fort at home. For your information, your rescue was a complete surprise to all of us. You are fortunate we found you. Besides, Wyle and I are already married. Mr. Hill performed the ceremony."

Wyle chuckled. "My apologies for not asking your permission, sir."

"Hmm, I'm not sure whether I should congratulate you, Wyle, or offer my condolences. Marian is a handful when she gets like this."

"Now that's settled, could we be on our way?" Marian asked. "I want to be at the count's house while it's still night. Back to the river before dawn would be even better."

The count's horses were not kites, especially the black brute that carried Wyle, so they made good time on the roads, but just when they were within a mile of Blaye, a troop of horse approached on the road from the south.

"Since I am wearing the only thing resembling a French uniform," Wyle said. "I suggest I tell them you are my prisoner, Major Greenway."

"In your deplorable French? Why don't we make a run for it?" Marian asked.

"I don't think either subterfuge will be necessary," said her father. "If I mistake not, those are English-shod horses."

"You can tell?" Wyle asked.

"Who goes there?" a voice shouted as the cavalry troop pulled up.

"Major Greenway of the Light Division, just released from a French prison by my intrepid daughter and son-in-law, Captain Wyle. Is that you, Digby?"

"Yes, sir, and glad to hear of your escape. We feared you were dead or worse."

"I must see these two to safety, and then I will be

rejoining my unit. If you encounter our dear general, you may tell him so."

"I shall deliver your message. Too bad you missed the last bit of fighting. Flogging the French ahead of us to Paris is no fun, though the wine is good."

"See you don't take a fall because of it. Carry on, Captain."

"Papa, do you really mean to stay and not even go home to Mother though she has not seen you in years?"

"She's a soldier's wife. She'll understand. Besides, I'm sure you'll say everything that's proper."

"Yes, you're not dead after all, and all your love. She'll be touched."

"Sir," Wyle protested, "you cannot be at full strength. I'm sure a leave would be granted if you asked."

"And miss everything? Elizabeth will understand. She can join me in Paris."

"Don't waste your breath, Wyle. He's beyond reason when he gets like this."

Her father and Wyle traded looks at this remark and laughed.

When they arrived at the house rented by Villars, it was in shambles, with the servants packing trunks and stacking them in the hall. Charlotte and Louisa were sitting on the sofa having tea and occasionally hugging each other, while everyone crowded in and the major was introduced.

The count rose painfully and came toward them. "So it is true. *La grande armée* is in retreat?"

"So it appears. We met a forerunner of British cavalry coming from Bordeaux," her father said as he sat and accepted a cup of tea from Louisa.

Villars shrugged. "I must try again to get passage for Louisa to England."

Marian nudged Wyle.

"Why don't you come with us, all of you?" Wyle suggested. "We slipped out of England. We may be able to get back in. Besides, I've been told my French is deplorable. You could increase our chances of getting Charlotte safely home."

"It is much to ask, but could you take care of Louisa for me until the war is over?"

Marian stepped forward. "Sir, you are far too injured to fight again, and the cause is lost. Please come with us yourself, and your servants. With no outbound cargo, we will have plenty of space."

"You are very generous, both of you, but duty—"

"Henri, come say goodbye to Charlotte. The major says they mean to be back at the river before dawn."

Marian noticed Wyle flinch. Louisa must have insisted on the name for his son.

"Your duty is to them," Marian said to Villars.

"Not to put too fine a point on it," Greenway said, "as the ranking British officer in the town, it would be my duty to take you prisoner and compel you to come with us."

Villars laughed almost with relief and undid the tassel of his sword.

"Keep your saber, sir. We all may have need of it. I see the carriage is still here. How soon may we be ready?"

Villars glanced around the room. "With the packing finished, I should say we could leave almost instantly."

Marian reached her arm around Wyle's waist and hugged him. "I don't think you can help being a hero."

He smiled down at her. "But I would like to give it a rest for a time."

# Chapter Fourteen

"You could at least untie me," protested Cole. Now that he was conscious, he was sitting upright on top of the coach but still bound at the hands.

"And have you use your men to take us prisoner?" Marian said from horseback. "That would be stupid indeed."

"I would give you my word."

"You kidnapped three people dear to me and probably would have murdered all of them if it had suited your purpose. Don't speak to me about honor."

"You obviously mean to go back on your word."

"How so? We have no liking for the gossip that would issue if we had you charged with your crimes. You will be set free when we are safely landed in England. But I'd be stupid to free you until we are there. So don't throw any rubs in the way of the voyage."

The wizened coachman and his ancient horses set them down at the river, haggled for more pay—after all, he had been tied up—which Marian granted him. As soon as the coach was unloaded, he left them. The two sailors from the ship's longboat were too drunk to row, so Wyle and Greenway laid them out on the dock and helped Charlotte, Louisa, and the count into the boat. Several small trunks contained all their baggage. The two French serving men took over the oars and Louisa's maid crouched over the jewelry box. Hill held the tie rope and Wyle waited for Marian, who stood on the shore with her father.

"I'm glad the count was willing to sell you his horses since you are determined to be back in the fray."

"I'm glad Wyle is letting him escape to England. He's not a bad fellow for a Frenchman."

"You will be careful? Mother will never forgive me if anything happens to you at this point."

"The war is nearly over. She would never expect me to miss the best part. Kiss her for me." Greenway embraced his daughter and pecked her cheek. "And take care of the estate till I get back." He mounted and rode away then with his new spare mounts in tow.

When they had rowed out to the ship, the real haggling began. The first mate, seeing Cole a captive, was disinclined to take him on but finally agreed to have him as a passenger only. Cole roared like a scalded pig over this, but a passage was finally agreed, with the understanding that the first mate would captain the ship. Marian did not care about anything except getting to England.

She was wrong about there not being a cargo. The hold was packed with wine and brandy, which the crew had started to sample in Cole's absence. While the count and Charlotte helped Louisa to the captain's cabin, Wyle and Hill had to help the crew hoist the sails, with Marian translating the mate's orders. Cole was fuming on the afterdeck while the mate steered.

Several hours later, Marian came up the gangway with mugs of coffee for Wyle, the mate, and Hill, who happened to be steering at the moment under the tutelage of the first mate. Of course Hill's French was perfectly adequate, though his accent was deplorable. Wyle moved toward the prow and settled on a grating there with Marian beside him. The day was as fair as the wind. It wasn't exactly blowing to their advantage, but if they tacked into it, they would reach home in a few days.

"The weather is calmer than I expected," she said.

"Are Charlotte and Louisa sleeping?"

"No, still talking, and the count as well. They have a lot of catching up to do."

"What a mad adventure. Who would have thought we'd find your father, too?"

"It makes sense, when I think back on it. Cole was looking for Papa to kill him, but the more I refused him, the less confident he was that his ace would work. He decided to hold Papa in reserve as a lever and abduct the children. What better way to lure me to France, and he could have his revenge on you into the bargain."

"And if you had willingly wed Cole in England?"

"He would have executed Papa, but your family would have been safe."

"I tend to think marriage to you would not have been the fulfilling experience your cousin expected. What will you do with him?"

Marian felt his arm snake around her waist and recalled that they were man and wife. If only there was one cabin on the ship where they might act on that. "Not prosecute. We don't want the scandal. I worry that news of Charlotte's disappearance will cause remark enough. If she had social ambitions, this could well ruin them." She glanced down at the skirt she had donned again. But her breeches were still underneath, in case there should be another emergency.

"Yes, Louisa's flight from me was almost enough."

She glanced sideways at him. "Of course, there is

always Mr. Hill."

"Why are you looking at me like that? If they choose to marry, I will approve."

"Because you never looked any higher for Charlotte yourself."

Wyle sighed and hugged her. "You have guessed she is Villars' daughter."

"Yes, there is a resemblance, especially in the eyes, which could be noted by anyone who sees them together."

"Who in society will ever see them together?"

"Probably no one. Does Hill know?"

"I plan to tell him if it becomes necessary."

"It won't make a bit of difference to him."

"I don't think so either. I see no need to tell Charlotte. If she guesses someday, then she will have two fathers. The count has agreed to be my estate manager. Old Clawson can teach him the ropes and retire as he has planned these five years."

"You seem to be putting a lot of faith into the man who enticed Louisa away."

"It was I who stole his wife, though I did not know it at the time. Louisa's parents were desperate to get her safely out of France, so they arranged our marriage. I realized she had come to me pregnant but could forgive her that. What I did not know was that she had married Villars in a private ceremony. When it turned out he was not killed in battle, she returned to him."

"The child was a girl."

"Even if it had been a boy I would have claimed him." He drained the tin mug and put it down. "You know what I'm talking about. There is something so particularly fragile about her that you can't help feeling sorrow for her."

"And love?"

"No, there was never any love between us, just need and compassion. It turns out that isn't enough for a marriage."

"And what about us, now that the war is over?"

"What do you mean? We are married and will be again after the ball." He kissed her on the lips.

"Will you resign your commission?"

"I already have."

"When?"

"That last day I went to Woolwich. When I saw how unhappy it made you, I simply made the decision. Or perhaps it was those nonsensical orders. The note made me miss our ride, and I was angry. Why are you looking at me like that?"

"So you sold out before we were married."

"Yes, of course. It's what I promised."

"Why didn't you tell me?"

"In all the excitement of leaving you in charge, I guess I just forgot. Who is in charge now, by the way?"

"I told you. My mother."

"That's a relief. I had visions of Aunt Alva taking the helm."

"I wish I could warn Mother. This will come as almost as big a shock as Papa's disappearance."

"But a pleasant one. We are a ragtag group. You in that ripped and torn riding dress, me in a uniform I don't even deserve anymore, Hill wounded. And we will have to sneak the count and Louisa out to Fair Oaks."

"By what the crew tell me, it will be dark when they row us in, so no one will even notice."

"I find that I do not care who notices us anymore."

He pulled her to him for a kiss that caused the sailors on deck to whistle in appreciation. Hill and the mate chuckled at the wheel.

"Yes, life is all that matters. Though it would be well for us if we returned in time for Alva's ball. Oh, no!"

"What?"

"I have missed my fitting."

Wyle stared at her, then burst into laughter. Finally Marian saw the humor in it and joined him.

"And you thought you would be embarrassed if I decamped on the engagement. Your aunt is probably biting nails by now."

## Chapter Fifteen

Wyle adjusted his neckcloth and Alva tweaked Marian's gown as they formed up in the receiving line. "Not even a single fitting, but it looks well enough, I suppose. Wyle, why you had to career off to Fair Oaks with the ball only a week away is beyond me. And to take Mr. Hill with you was unconscionable. I had to make all the final arrangements myself."

"But Alva, you know you love to have a free hand with my ballroom. It's beautiful. Roses everywhere! Are there any left in the whole city?"

"A few. It's done now. We just have to greet the guests and behave with propriety. Charlotte, you are a vision."

Wyle smiled at his daughter in her white lawn with rose ribbons. She looked innocent, excited, dewy, and wonderful.

When Alva went to confer with Trumby, Marian whispered to Wyle, "I wish the count and Louisa could see Charlotte now."

"So do I, but they knew it would be fatal to appear with her, even under an assumed name. We were hoping people would get over the gossip of her abandonment. Seeing her would show the resemblance and ruin Charlotte's chances. They will be able to see her anytime they wish now, living in the dower house, and we will give a dinner at Fair Oaks where she can wear the dress again."

"I'm so glad you insisted they come to England."

"It's easy to be generous when you are already the happiest man on earth." He laced his fingers with hers and drew her hand up and kissed it. That is how the first of their well-wishers found them.

The dancing was a blur for Marian as she was introduced to one acquaintance after another. Cousins Bertram and Edward were both there and partnered her for a set each. Every time she glanced toward the dowager's corner, Charlotte dutifully waved, as did Aunt Flora. How dull for the child, but better than being excluded. Contrary to what Alva said about keeping Charlotte under her wing, she had convinced Flora to look after the girl while Alva worked her way around the room talking to everyone.

When Morris appeared and asked Marian to walk to the refreshment table set up in the breakfast parlor, she realized Isabelle and Sophie must have come after all. Alva had reported a flare-up between them but had not elaborated on the cause or upshot except that they would not attend.

"Mother is in a strange mood."

"How so?"

"She planned not to attend, but that moped Sophie so much she changed her mind. Still, I don't think she is fit company." He absently ladled two cups of punch and handed her one, glancing around to make sure they were not overheard.

"Will she say anything that will hurt Wyle?"

"What could she possibly say that would hurt him? He's a soldier. But you, well, I thought I should warn you. I have tried to reason with her, but she is convinced you are a fortune hunter who must be stopped."

Marian shrugged. "Just so you know, your mother and I have already had words. I told her that if she were a man I would call her out for some of the things she said."

"Ha, I bet that did not sit well. I wish I could stop her, but I thought I should at least warn you."

"Thank you, Morris. I wonder what made her decide to come. What does she know now that she did not before?"

"I think it has something to do with that pair of footmen she lent to help decorate the ballroom. When they returned, she interrogated them."

"And discovered what?"

"That you and Wyle had left the city together. At least that you were not here but that your mother was. Don't you see? If she tells people you went away with Wyle unchaperoned, your reputation will be ruined even if he does marry you. It's not fair, what she does to people."

"Thank you, Morris. I will never forget your loyalty in this matter. I must find Wyle."

"He was in the card room—the library."

She set out for the room named but stopped herself. This was no time to be pitching headlong into disaster.

"Wait," Morris said. "You should not fetch him. Let me."

"Would you? Ask him to meet me at the entrance to the dining room. It's almost time to go in to supper anyway."

When Wyle entered the ballroom and glanced about for Marian, the musicians had just finished a set and their rest signaled that supper was about to be served, that and

Trumby throwing the double doors open with his white-gloved hands. Morris had looked rattled just now, so Wyle had a feeling Marian needed more from him than his arm in to supper.

He made his way through the laughing crowd to Marian. "What is it?" he asked as he led her into the dining room. The room was packed with extra tables and chairs, and they had only a moment to talk before others surrounded them.

"Morris reports that his mother planted two spies in the household, a brace of footmen, who informed her we were both away for the best part of a week without Mother."

"That tears it. I thought some people were looking at me oddly."

"I have been getting the same sort of stares, but only after Isabelle arrived. I hope Aunt Flora takes Charlotte upstairs now. Things could get ugly."

"I saw them going. Look, there is Morris bringing your mother in to dinner."

"Whatever happens, Morris is our friend."

"And Aunt Alva has captured Mr. Hill for escort."

It took many minutes for the entire company to find seats. Alva had not invited three hundred after all, or at least no more than a hundred had come. The murmuring abated when Cousin Bertram rose to propose a toast to their engagement. It was a wonderful toast, full of well wishes that caused Isabelle to fume in her seat. Many ladies gazed at her with fascination as though watching a powder keg about to blow.

After they had all drunk, Wyle rose. "Thank you, Bertram Meecham, for that glowing sendoff, but I have to report that we are a sham."

Marian sucked in a breath, for this was the script of her nightmare, the one where Wyle called the engagement off.

Wyle reached for Marian's hand and pulled her up and to his side. "This wonderful lady became my wife well over a week ago by special license. In short, we eloped."

Peals of laughter were followed by applause and the clinking of glasses.

Edward rose unsteadily to his feet, crumpled the paper where he had writ the second toast and tossed it over his shoulder. "Congratulations, cuz, and to you, Lady Wyle, my condolences and hopes that you shall be able to manage this madman better than his family has."

"Thank you, Mr. Ridgeway. I am happy to call you cousin as well."

"It's a sham," Isabelle said.

Mr. Hill leaped to his feet. "I assure you they are man and wife, for I performed the ceremony myself with Lady Elizabeth as witness. Let me add my congratulations, sir, and to your lady as well."

"Lady?" Isabelle was on her feet now, her cheeks flaming as she shook off Sophie's restraining hand.

Morris raised his eyes to heaven in either fervent prayer or casting up all hope.

"There is nothing ladylike—"

"We should not omit the reason for the couple's so hasty elopement," the vibrant voice of Lady Elizabeth said.

Marian stared at her mother standing proudly before the group with a voice of command so marked that the room stilled. "We had word that my husband, Major Greenway, was held prisoner in a coastal town in France.

Lord Wyle engaged a ship, and because of her mastery of French my daughter thought it prudent to go with him as his wife. With the aid of Mr. Hill, they rescued Major Greenway. He is even now rejoining his troop and on the way to Paris to celebrate our victory over the French." She held up her glass.

With this announcement, a mass of cheering erupted and more than one glass met its tinkling end with the resulting toast. Marian glanced at Isabelle, who fled the ballroom. Sophie was about to follow her when Morris slid closer to her and whispered encouragement in her ear. Marian smiled at the girl, and she sniffed and nodded. At least they could keep these two in the fold even if Isabelle chose to disgrace herself.

Several hours later, Wyle led both Marian and her mother up the stairs. "That was masterful, Lady Elizabeth. You could have had every male in attendance signed up to go off to war if you had continued."

"I spoke no more than the truth."

"But not all of it, fortunately," Marian said. "By directing attention toward Papa, no one even thought about Charlotte."

"Yes, your father. He had better come home unscathed or I'll kill him myself." She whisked into her room and left the couple laughing in the hall.

"And now, my lady. Shall we?"

"We must hold the record for the longest wait between wedding and bedding."

He paused to kiss her on the threshold of his suite. "And it was well worth the wait, every moment of it."

## Chapter Sixteen

Marian came out the back door of Fair Oaks and crossed the stone patio, carrying a letter which she read as she walked. She almost tripped on the blanket spread on the grass where Wyle lounged eating a bowl of grapes while he watched Hill, Charlotte, Henry, the count, and Louisa playing croquet.

The children had not been shocked that their mother was still alive, since her faked death had not seemed real to them. They had spent more time with her now that she was happy than they ever had when she was tortured by grief and regret. They got on quite well with her and the count.

"News from the front?"

"Mother has finally caught up to Papa in Paris. This time she vows she will bring him home, but she sounds happy." Marian sank down beside him and he put a grape into her mouth.

"So it all turned out well, almost like a fairy tale."

"Against all odds and mostly by chance, yes, we are all as happy as we can possibly be in a world ravaged by war. Oh, here is a letter for you."

"This must be from Frobisher." He popped the seal. "But not our little corner of it. And it wasn't by chance that your father advised me to trust you. He was right. You are equal to anything."

"I certainly hope so. What news?"

"They actually saw a bit of action and acquitted themselves well. They remain in Paris. He's sorry I missed all the excitement. Hah! If only he knew."

Hill and Charlotte approached him shyly, she with excitement writ large on her face.

"Sir, I fear I have presumed beyond my station," he said.

"Father, must I have a come-out? Can I not just marry Lewis now rather than waiting for the season? His father wants to perform the rite."

"Sir, I spoke ahead of myself."

"Easy, Hill. Do you really think I would have dangled you in front of my daughter without the hope that you two would one day make a match of it? Charlotte, you have my leave to marry from the schoolroom if you wish. This will chagrin Cousin Isabelle, who would have delighted to show Sophie off at your come-out ball."

Hill looked surprised, then relieved.

"I don't care for such stuff," Charlotte said.

Marian smiled. "You will be a hit anyway, and we will have a ball after your wedding just like your father and I had. You will be the most beautiful young matron of the season. Poets will swoon over their lost chance with you."

"Perhaps I will be with child by then and can give the whole thing a miss. Come, Lewis, we must tell your parents." Charlotte ran off before either of them could comment on her indelicate remark. Hill flushed and ran after her.

Now Henry trudged toward them. "The game is falling apart. Mother is going off with Charlotte talking about dresses, but the count promised to teach me fencing. Is that all right? I mean, I know he's French, but he doesn't seem like the enemy."

"By all means. The man has the patience of a saint, so I'm sure he will do well with you. But do not tax his arm. It has only started to heal properly."

The count waved and went off toward the stable with Henry, who was answering him in broken French.

"Well, Captain Wyle. The field is ours. Perhaps we should just wait the season out here." She lay back with her head in his lap, hoping for another grape.

"You were never one to flaunt your victory, but why so shy of the *ton*?"

"Even if Charlotte will not be increasing by then, I am. All those balls might interfere with feeding the baby."

He gasped and laid his ruined right hand over her still flat stomach. He did it reverently as though he could not believe his good fortune. "One thing every commander learns is to communicate the position to us poor subalterns as soon as she knows it. Why didn't you tell me?"

"I wanted to wait for the right moment or when we even had a spare moment. Our life is almost as busy now as before we came to Fair Oaks. Even after we were married, we had very little time together, with the preparations for the ball. Then you had to ruin it by announcing we had eloped and married."

"Only to keep Isabelle from defaming you. Besides, we thus avoided another round of parties."

"True. I fear we will become hermits here. Never have I enjoyed a place so much."

"Not even your own home?" he asked.

"That was always work, with the specter of Cole

looming over me. He ruined it for me. But Mother will put it to rights and file an action against the solicitor who overstepped his bounds. I find myself in awe of her penchant for justice."

"You didn't tell her we let your cousin go?"

"No. I'd rather think of him scrabbling for a living than disgracing us."

"I have not seen that prim governess face for weeks now. I rather enjoyed that disapproving scowl from time to time. It made me sit up and take notice."

"I'm through with playing a part. I'll save the stern face for our children when they have disobeyed us."

He drew her into his arms and kissed her, knowing that life with Marian might be fraught with schedules and lessons but it would never be dull. And now there would be more children. He relished the role of father even more than he'd liked the job of soldiering. He would be creating rather than destroying.

And he thought their brood would be lively and intelligent. Would they all have Marian's penchant for throwing herself into danger?

It would be interesting to find out.

## A word about the author...

Barbara Jean Miller has mentored in the Writing Popular Fiction Masters Program at Seton Hill University since its inception in 1999. She writes in several genres but her favorite is historical romantic suspense. She calls them action/adventure romances with the heroine sharing in the struggles and rescue in equal parts with the hero. These struggles often involve mysteries and horses.

Barb lives with her husband and pets on an ancient farm in Western Pennsylvania which contributes authentic settings to her novels.

https://barbarajeanmiller.substack.com

www.ingramcontent.com/pod-product-compliance
Lightning Source LLC
Chambersburg PA
CBHW070502260626
47161CB00004B/1421